"In Cole Ryerson . . . R. C. House has created a memorable Man of the Old West. House's work gets better with each book. . . ."

—Dale L. Walker, president of the Western Writers of America, *Rocky Mountain News*

STOUTHEARTED MEN

U.S. MARSHAL COLE RYERSON: For years, Bad-Face Ike has been a thorn in the marshal's side. Now, this hard-driving lawman has vowed to bring Ike down at any cost. . . .

BAD-FACE IKE BODENE: They've yet to build the jail that can hold this rampaging half-breed killer. Ike's given the ultimate challenge to Ryerson: Catch me—if you can. . . .

"Marshal Cole Ryerson is cast in the mold of John Wayne's Rooster Cogburn. . . . With the death of Louis L'Amour, there is a need for somebody to fill the vacuum. . . . One of the established writers who will claim his share of the range is undoubtedly R. C. House."

—Don Coldsmith, Spur Award–winning
author of *The Spanish Bit Saga*

❖

STOUTHEARTED MEN

CACTUS JACK MAGUIRE: Cole Ryerson's young *segundo* gave his life to the law and his love to one woman. But he could lose both in the hunt for Ike Bodene. . . .

BERTHA MAGUIRE: Wise to the ways of the West, Cactus Jack's wife knew the Lord and the law giveth —and taketh away. Yet that won't keep her from speaking her piece. . . .

"House captures that time after the Civil War when bold men ventured westward. . . . You can smell burnt powder, taste the trail dust."

—Jory Sherman, Spur Award–winning
author of *The Medicine Horn*

STOUTHEARTED MEN

DR. HANS SEABRING: An astronomer who's been through many earthly conflagrations. The former Prussian army officer dreams of the stars but keeps his telescope trained on Bad-Face Ike. . . .

SPUNKY SMITH: After five years, he's riding again with Marshal Ryerson. This is the toughest manhunt of Spunky's career, and one mistake could end it all. . . .

"CAP" DONOVAN: Cap was once the pride of the Texas Rangers, and his white hair can't quell the fiery spirit that's made him, at the age of seventy-four, one of Ryerson's Renegades. . . .

Books by R. C. House

Stouthearted Men*
Verdict at Medicine Springs*
Ryerson's Manhunt*
Spindrift Ridge*
Requiem for a Rustler*
Warhawk
Trackdown at Immigrant Lake*
Drumm's War (with Bill Bragg)
The Sudden Gun
Vengeance Mountain
So the Loud Torrent

*Published by POCKET BOOKS

R. C. HOUSE

STOUTHEARTED MEN

A COLE RYERSON NOVEL

POCKET BOOKS

New York London Toronto Sydney Tokyo Singapore

This book is a work of fiction. Names, characters, places and incidents are products of the author's imagination or are used fictitiously. Any resemblance to actual events or locales or persons, living or dead, is entirely coincidental.

An *Original* Publication of POCKET BOOKS

POCKET BOOKS, a division of Simon & Schuster Inc.
1230 Avenue of the Americas, New York, NY 10020

ISBN: 0-671-87245-1

First Pocket Books printing March 1995

10 9 8 7 6 5 4 3 2 1

POCKET and colophon are registered trademarks of Simon & Schuster Inc.

Cover art by Tim Tanner

Printed in the U.S.A.

STOUTHEARTED
MEN

1

A killer and pillager deluxe named Bad-Face Ike Bodene broke jail for the second time and is on the prod. That's why I called together this *posse comitatus* of stouthearted men. There'll be six of us against about three to one odds."

U.S. Marshal Cole Ryerson spoke firmly and directly, determined to pull no punches. It was part of his well-planned scheme to fuse the assembled manhunters into a fearless—and peerless—tracking and fighting unit.

He leaned forward, planting his hands against the mahogany rim and green felt cushion of the billiard table in the back room of McCurdy's Saloon in Fort Walker, New Mexico, and studied the faces of each of them momentarily. That intensity, too, would hold their attention and build their suspense.

The place was poorly lit and reeked of cue chalk, carelessly emptied spittoons, and dense cigarette smoke.

1

Ryerson made a grim set to his eyes and mouth; no point in letting any of them think this would be a Sunday school picnic. Each was an old friend and trusted ally—but virtual strangers to one another.

Ryerson's deliberate and weighted pauses gave Sylvester "Spunky" Smith, his old deputy from San Patricio, a chance to study Ryerson in light of the five years since they'd last met.

He was the same Boot Hill Cole of the old days, but wearing a black broadcloth suit now instead of knockabout range clothes. The only indication of the passage of years and the piling on of age showed in his lightly grizzled sideburns and a creeping carelessness about his dress; his suit hadn't been cleaned or pressed in weeks.

Spunky knew that the silver-haired, durable-looking old jasper next to him must be the former Texas Ranger captain, Jeremiah "Cap" Donovan. It was Cap, Spunky knew, who'd taught Ryerson the law-keeping ropes in Texas twenty years before when Ryerson—barely into his twenties—was a newly discharged veteran of four fierce years as a cavalry officer under his all-time hero, Confederate General Joseph Orville Shelby of Missouri.

Newest of the bunch, Spunky also knew, was the lean kid beside him watching Ryerson intently. He would be Cactus Jack Maguire, the deputy marshal who'd lately backed Ryerson's plays in bringing scalawags and scofflaws to the bar of justice of elderly Federal Judge Isaac Winfield, legendary as the Lion of Fort Walker, and Ryerson's number two hero.

"The jail ain't made, it seems," Ryerson continued,

"that can hold that damned breed Bodene. That, or the jailer ain't been born that can't be buffaloed by the likes of this character Bad-Face Ike. I've seen to puttin' him away twice at great hazard to life and limb. Then somehow those jailers turn their backs, and that slippery little jasper is gone like smoke. Last time he broke jail, he put together a gang of cutthroats, renegades, killers, and comancheros that'll match any ever in the West when it comes to doing evil and transgressing against the word of the Lord or the acts of Congress!"

When he wanted to, Spunky thought, Cole Ryerson could match any stump speaker or fire-and-brimstone preacher.

"Three weeks ago, Ike's gang stopped the eastbound Southern and Central Railroad train thirty or so miles south of here and hit the express car for ten thousand dollars in cash, gold specie, and negotiable banknotes."

Ryerson warmed to his speech, and his five old cronies basked in an excited glow with occasional grunts of anticipation and visceral chuckles of manhunter zeal. "I tracked you all down to conduct the most important manhunt of my career. I have every intention of bringing in this brazen outlaw for good and all. It's my fondest hope that Mr. Bodene gives us just cause to return him back here to justice dead-stiff as a horse collar over his own saddle. In other words, I am not fixing to go after Bad-Face Ike again in this life."

Ryerson backed away from the billiard table to pace back and forth between it and a row of high stools for observers and wall-mounted racks of public cue sticks.

"You are all my close friends, each of you for various reasons, but each of you dedicated to the causes of justice. I'll manage proper introductions shortly.

"Meanwhile, to demonstrate the extreme gravity of our enterprise, I have here a note spirited to me by person or persons unknown on behalf of Mr. Ike Bodene."

Ryerson struggled with his clothing to fish in the inside breast pocket of his broadcloth coat. He unfurled a small rectangle of worn and gray foolscap.

"Ike has hurled down the challenge, has called me out. A note that suggests not only has he made himself rich with the Southern and Central haul but he knows that I'll again be on his trail and taunts me into one last showdown."

He allowed a heavy silence to fall over the expectant men facing him. He clumped over to the room's only window to study the letter in better light, which was only a sickly yellow glare. A liberal dusting of fine decomposed desert granite outside and an oily nicotine film inside rendered a hazy translucence to the small, segmented panes already flawed with wavy imperfections.

"It's right here in Ike's own hand," Ryerson continued, holding the paper at arm's length to read. "That son of a bitch also despises my guts for past interferences into the conduct of his normal course of thievery and mayhem. It says right here that if I take out after him, he proposes to set every manner of trap and

4

guile to snare me with the expressed intent, if I interpret his words correctly—and in fact the solemn promise—to feed my mortal body to the wolves . . ."

He paused again for effect, sending a flinty scowl at the five still standing in the weak light around the pool table.

"*. . . One piece at a time!*"

Somebody gasped, "Aw-oh!" It brought a moment of tension that was broken by some deep-throated and sardonic chortles; to Cole Ryerson such a threat was tantamount to waving a red flag at a bull.

Ryerson continued his pacing, his stubby thick wooden boot heels a series of ominous thuds in the tight silence of the pool room floor.

"Of course, I am not in the least intimidated by Mr. Ike Bodene, that offal-eating bastard. But I figured going up against fifteen to twenty by ourselves was a pretty big chunk of possum meat for just me and Mr. Maguire to bite off alone.

"So, to the best of my knowledge, I have sent for my most trusted and expert friends spanning twenty or so years of law-keeping. All of you have ridden or otherwise been associated with me in the causes of justice and domestic tranquillity. You all know of one another by reputation but have not met until today.

"Now I've not gotten you here on the basis of friendship alone. There is a significant bounty on the head of Bad-Face Ike Bodene which will be share and share alike among *you*. I only want the little bastard's brown hide tacked to the main gate of Fort Walker which, of course, is nonexistent, but you catch my drift. I have no doubt that Ike's saddle mates also have

5

circulars around for their apprehension. I'm headed on a hunting trip, gentlemen, and I wanted to share the spoils with the finest and greatest trackers and manhunters any lawman has been privileged to know and work with."

He hesitated. "But I'll settle for you all instead."

Again he paused, this time like a comic actor as he waited for a hearty round of laughter to die down. "When the court determines a just bounty for their hides, those who are blessed with returning will reap handsomely."

Done with the preliminaries, Ryerson stepped back to the billiard table's rim and again leaned forward, bracing his hands against it.

"You'll all be duly sworn, of course. Mainly because he knows the territory better than any of you, my present deputy will be my *segundo,* Cactus Jack Maguire, who's been my second in command here at Fort Walker now three years."

Ryerson was always careful to properly acknowledge his active and former associates and protégés and give their law-keeping roles and performance proper acknowledgment and respect; it was another trait that built unswerving loyalty in the men who rode with him.

"Mr. Maguire knows Ike Bodene well, having helped me subdue the chili-eating bastard before his latest jailbreak. As my alternate, Mr. Maguire has gained a proficiency with firearms to become a crack shot with a Winchester at long range and with a Colt at man-stopping distance. Mr. Maguire, front and center, and comment if you will."

6

The l...
past Spunk...
take his place...
advanced in ran...
company command...
Spunky figured he'd ge...
birds of a feather, and Magu...
qualities.

Facing the posse men, Maguire ...
face, but an expression that spoke o... ...stei
tence if and when it was called for. There
leanness of jaw and a set of eye that inspired trust i...
one so young. He was skinny, but with the mettle of a
steel trap, his clothing fresh-laundered, starched and
pressed, clearly the work of a dedicated wife.

"I've not much to add, Mr. Ryerson," Maguire
began, and Spunky's mistrust grew; he'd heard that
line before. "Like Mr. Ryerson says, this Bodene is an
ornery *hombre.*" Maguire pronounced "ornery" as
though it was "on-ree." "This *posse comitatus* consists
of six men, including Marshal Ryerson. That means
we're outnumbered on the order of two or three to
one." Maguire liked the lilt of his words, so he said it
again, with emphasis. "On the order of two or three to
one."

Ryerson beamed with uncommon pride at his
young protégé. "And in this business, those are normal or better odds," he added.

"Yes," Maguire went on. "From what I've heard of
you gentlemen who've rode with Mr. Ryerson, those
aren't odds you're unfamiliar or uncomfortable
with."

glow of kind words,
his estimate of Cactus Jack,

to what we'll get into. We'll travel through
try, so chaps or canvas dusters are advised.
boots. Don't wear nothing unless you're
ed to waste them."

unky grimaced, wishing now that the kid would
off his soapbox; all this was chaff to men who'd
dden the trail after owlhoots most of their lives,
much of the time with Ryerson.

Maguire's words continued to hound him.

"We'll be long hours in the saddle, and Mr. Ryerson
and I hope none of you has lately suffered inguinal
hernia."

Ryerson cleared his throat and stepped forward.
"Yeah, any of you been ruptured since I saw you last?
Speak now and you'll be excused but still in line for
your share of the bounty."

The strangers around the billiard table looked at
each other, grinning and snickering—a response in
the negative.

"For those who get gallt from the saddle or gets an
attack of the piles, Mrs. Maguire, my wife, Bertha, has
put up a goodly amount of her own homemade
medicinal salve. Anybody who gets those complaints,
see me. I guess that's all, Mr. Ryerson."

Ryerson put a hand on Maguire's shoulder in
appreciation as well as a gentle shove back to his place
beside the table before he resumed.

"Thank you, Mr. Maguire. Oh, by the way, gents, he
goes by Cactus Jack, for those who didn't know. And
because a trip like this involves some risk to human

hide and bone, we've pretty complete home medical gear with us, courtesy of the wife of Cactus Jack."

Ryerson again studied the faces watching him closely. "Mrs. Maguire is a very thorough woman. A very thorough woman, indeed!"

Maguire took his place, trying to act casual by parking one side of his rump and thigh on the table's rim, but Spunky glimpsed a kind of embarrassed grimace at Ryerson's comment. It might, Spunky mused, be an indication that Cactus Jack was henpecked.

Still, men showed different faces in differing situations. Cactus Jack was probably no exception. Tough as nails and would never back down when it came to an encounter with a hard case, but meek as a lamb in the privacy of his own sitting room under the stern glare of a demanding wife. Ryerson's voice intruded.

"I guess my third in command is that there young Mex. Show your colors, Fernando!"

The greasy-haired, olive-complexioned character with the sharp sweat aroma hovering about him next to Spunky raised his shoulders and looked around in the self-conscious response of a Mexican among a gang of gringos. Feeling everyone's eyes on him, he slouched again in embarrassment.

"Now Fernando there," Ryerson went on, "once was on a par with Bad-Face Ike Bodene. A turn in Yuma Prison rendered him a right proper cut above. Fernando'll be chief scout and meat-hunter this trip. He can track a snail over creek ice and hit his mark with a .44 Winchester where he aims at two hundred yards. And only slightly wide of the mark at five hundred. He'll be gone a lot pokin' ahead, lookin' to cut the sign of Ike's bunch. When he knows he's in the free and clear—out of earshot of the *hombres* we're hunting—Fernando'll watch for meat for the camp pot. We travel simple, gentlemen. Short rations, as always. But we'll feast regular and well on fresh meat. And when the evening pipe is lit, I've arranged for a goodly measure of what we used to call forty-rod whiskey to ease the saddle cramps and settle full bellies. Thanks for comin' along, Fernando."

Encouraged by Ryerson's praise, Fernando proudly rose to his full height and tossed a ragged salute in appreciation of Ryerson's words. Spunky knew by reputation that Fernando was the product of several generations of mergers of Mexicans and Indians, belligerent Yaquis, for sure, and devil-may-care Spanish Conquistadores. Only a generation before, his mother was the issue of a black prostitute and a white adventurer. In Spunky's eyes, Fernando was southwestern to the core.

"I go to jail because Meester Ryerson he put me there," Fernando confessed in a rare moment of openness, stumbling on in his crude English. "I deserve it but Meester Ryerson no kill me. He could, you know. When I leave Yuma Prison, I track Meester Ryerson and ask him for *trabajo*—work. He make me scout, hunter, pay good money. I send money to my family in Mexico. Now I big man in my village, like *alcalde*. I never let Meester Ryerson down, I tell you this."

Fernando was obviously flustered by his revelations and stepped back quickly out of whatever limelight the darkened room afforded. He again looked around self-consciously, as though expecting criticism. When he found only approving glances, Fernando relaxed and leaned against the billiard table.

A vigorous rap on the door to the saloon resounded hollowly in the darkened room as though sounding an alarm; Ryerson stepped into the deeper shadows, his form briefly backlit by the late afternoon rectangle of sunbeam through the window reflecting on the ever-present dust motes.

At least five of the six right arms—including Ryerson's—bent almost automatically, raising palms and flexed fingers closer to the sinister butts of holstered six-guns. The air around them turned tense.

"Easy, boys," Ryerson called hoarsely. Then louder, "Yeah! Who's there? This is a private meeting!"

Door hinges wheezed as they parted a fraction of an inch, letting in a thin band of light from the saloon.

"Ryerson? Winfield."

"Judge? Come in, sir!"

The door opened fully to admit a man who, by appearances, could have been Methuselah's grandfather. Thinned, shrunken, and stooped with advanced age, the well-dressed man in a dark suit and string bow tie shuffled in, clutching a sheaf of papers.

His full head of uncommonly thick, snow white hair flowed back from his forehead and around his ears like the mane of a lion; his dark, alert eyes also held the intense glitter of a beast of the jungle. His aged shuffle surprisingly agile, he moved quickly toward Ryerson.

"Cole, I wanted to meet the members of your *posse comitatus* before you men got away. I also have issued bench warrants for Ike Bodene in particular and up to twenty John Does—the gang members not specifically identified, to those of you unfamiliar with lawyer talk. Thus, there will be no question of the legality of your arrests."

"That may turn out to be of great help, Judge," Ryerson said. "Gentlemen," he continued, addressing the five still in position around the pool table, "you've all heard of Judge Isaac Winfield, known in some quarters as 'the Lion of Fort Walker.'"

The wrinkled and shiny parchmentlike skin of the judge's face took on more creases in a smile of recognition, and he nodded several times toward the posse men.

"Judge," Ryerson began, "you know my deputy, Mr. John Maguire, yonder. Fellas, raise your hand when I call your name. Judge Winfield, you've heard me tell of my onetime deputy, Sylvester Smith. Take a bow, Spunky. Next to him, with hair maybe not quite as white as yours, is my very old friend, Captain Jeremiah Donovan, late of the great Texas Rangers. I daresay, too, that Cap's about a match for you in age. What are you now, Cap? Seventy-two?"

"Seventy-four!" Donovan barked. He seemed about to say more, but let it go at that.

"Across on the other side of the table is my young Mexican friend, Fernando. By the way, Judge, Fernando holds no grudge that you and I put him away in Yuma for a spell about five years back."

Fernando grinned at the judge and ducked his head self-consciously.

"I remember Fernando," Judge Winfield said, beaming. "I'm proud he's seen the light."

"And last, but surely not least," Ryerson continued, "is our scientist and astronomer friend, Dr. Hans

Seabring. I've told you a peck of lies about him, too. His fighting abilities were honed in the ranks of the Prussian army before he got smart and went away to college."

Ryerson had a peculiar way of pronouncing Hans, sounding like "Honce."

The slightly built man with the squat straw hat and peculiar oval spectacles clipped to his nose brought up his hand in a wave at the judge.

Judge Winfield stepped away from Ryerson to get closer to the posse men.

"Thank you, Marshal Ryerson. Now, then, gentlemen," he began in a voice remarkably strong for a man of his feeble appearance, "my comments will be brief so that you may get on with your deliberations. Strict adherence to the law has been the meat of my life. Therefore, my attitude should be to encourage you to bring in these recalcitrants alive to stand before the bar of justice. But the depravity of Mr. Ike Bodene and his contempt for jurisprudence prompts me to advise you that you'll suffer no reproach from me if you . . ."

The Lion of Fort Walker drew himself up to as much height as his rickety structure would allow; his eyes flashed, and his voice rang with new intensity.

". . . shoot every one of the sons of bitches down dead like a dog and drag 'em in tied over their saddles! Good day and good hunting, gentlemen!"

Judge Winfield handed his sheaf of papers to Ryerson and hurriedly shuffled out of the room.

"Thanks, Judge," Ryerson called after him as the door to the saloon closed with a resounding slam.

He turned back to his posse. "That pretty much

sums it up, gents. The official send-off. These papers also authorize me to deputize each of you for this expedition. We ride at first light in front of the courthouse prepared to go to any lengths to bring Ike's gang to account for its transgressions."

Ryerson fished out a silver-case watch as large as a turnip from his vest and thumbed open the hunting case. "Meanwhile, in an hour and twenty minutes, Mrs. Cactus Jack is preparing for us a fine feast of roast beef and all the trimmings. She is a thorough woman, as I can testify, having bellied up to her table more than a little. It will be a splendid meal.

"I suggest you all repair to your respective lodgings and refresh for the evening. Best bib and tucker to show due respect to the dear Mrs. Maguire. But at precisely five o'clock, twenty minutes from now, the drinks are on me in McCurdy's Saloon room yonder. Mrs. Maguire is a staunch Baptist and takes a dim view of spirited libations in her home.

"Twenty minutes back here at McCurdy's, gentlemen!"

2

With dawn, night clouds turned themselves into glorious smears of rose paint against a gray sky fast ripening to a rich blue along the eastern horizon. Close to the still-dark land, silhouetted forms of six mounted figures loomed black as paper cutouts against the dim of daybreak, their heads bobbing sleepily on the trail out of Fort Walker.

Two of the figures moving through the dark shroud of night-damp cold held the lead ropes to heavily loaded packhorses. Behind them, the oldest and the youngest—Cap Donovan and Cactus Jack Maguire—wrangled, urged, and otherwise hazed forward a remuda of relief mounts for each rider.

In the point position, under his massive black Stetson and with his split-tailed tan duster nearly covering Jo Shelby's flanks, rode Marshal Cole Ryerson. On the first day's march, Ryerson had chosen Spunky Smith as his point mate on his cutting horse and bred-for-the-trail mount, Old Stockholder.

"I'll ride point every day," Ryerson had told them in the chill dark at three in the morning as they gathered, prepared to ride, at the Fort Walker courthouse. "If old Ike lays a bushwhack, I'll be the most vulnerable. It's me he's after anyway, and I don't intend any of you to take a blue whistler destined for me. But since Ike has no desire to kill me outright and deprive himself of his heinous delights, point could very well be the safest place for any of you. I'll alternate my point-riding associate by the day. This will minimize the threat to each of you.

"Two of you will lead the pack animals each day, and we'll shift horse-wrangler duties daily as well."

Spunky, his night-dulled head nodding with sleep or concurrence with Ryerson in the morning cold—nonetheless feeling exhilaration at the start of the manhunt—allowed that was a pretty thoughty scheme. Ryerson, in a quarter-century of law-keeping, had mostly worked solo or with just one deputy. Having assembled a team now, Ryerson appeared to organize the affair along the lines of military tactics he'd been exposed to in four years of arduous service during the late war. In those days, Ryerson had skirmished in Arkansas, Missouri, and the Indian Nations under such legendary Rebel generals as Kirby Smith (who Spunky knew he was shirttail related to), "Old Pap" Sterling Price, and that gritty, celebrated old curmudgeon, General Jo Shelby, Ryerson's hero and commanding officer, as well as the namesake of the animal Ryerson bragged on as the finest horse any man had ever straddled.

Heading out, Spunky took his assigned place as

Ryerson's first-day point-riding associate, understanding that he'd have other duties for the next four days before he was back up front again with Ryerson.

By then, Spunky figured, they'd better have scented Ike Bodene or Ryerson would have boiled up a fine dose of the fantods for himself. By then, too, Spunky thought, he'd have at least a better grip on how all this was going to go.

The sun, growing in its brutality, quickly wiped away the morning mists and pleasantries to bore in by eight o'clock; and by ten a yellow malevolence rained down on the six and their dozen riding mounts and pack animals, the alkaline dust churning up around them like wraiths of poisonous vapor.

Riding along, separated from Ryerson and his other saddle mates in the defensive formation, Spunky eyed a distant, low-lying, sawtooth-peaked horizon undulating in shimmery mirage. Ryerson remained annoyingly chipper despite the grinding heat, seeming to relish being in command of a unit of stouthearted fighting men again.

"Outnumbered as we are," Ryerson shouted for all to hear, "our advantage is in our defensive conduct. Proved in military combat and in backwoods skirmishes. Straight out of 'Hardee's Tactics,' the bible of the fighting officers of both sides in the War between the States, and 'Rogers's Regulations for Rangers.' In our case, mostly the teachings of Colonel Robert Rogers.

"Rogers was the father of hit-and-run combat tactics in the 1750s," Ryerson proclaimed, pulling himself taller in the saddle. "Though created in the days of musketry—one shot before the reloading process, for those of you who never handled a muzzle-loader— Colonel Robert Rogers's Regulations set the tone for frontier-style combat for the wars and skirmishes that came after the French and Indian War. Wound up in 1763 to be exact.

"About a hundred years later in what some called the War for Southern Independence, Major Clayton— he was from Texas—gave written tests on Hardee and Rogers to us brevet officers. In the field, mind you! At night, after a day of fightin'! Most Yankees think the Confederacy was a gang of disorganized rabble. But under Shelby, we were a well-trained unit . . . not only to fight and command but to conduct a campaign.

"I can hear Major Clayton yet. He could quote chapter and verse from Rogers's Regulations. Got to where I near could, too. Let's see.

"It was Regulation Number Two that applies to us just now. 'If your number be small, march in a single file, keeping at such distance from each other as to prevent one shot from killing two men, sending one man or more forward, and the like on each side, at the distance of twenty yards from the main body, if the ground you march over will admit of it, to give the signal to the officer of the approach of the enemy, and of their number, et cetera . . .'"

Ryerson twisted in the saddle, studying his troops like a first-class commanding officer. Satisfied as to their strategic placement on the march, he turned back to face the enemy, or at least in the direction that enemy was thought to be.

Ryerson, Spunky knew, had been breveted a captain after two years of moving up in grade from private to sergeant major, mostly because of a galloping attrition that showed up best in battlefield casualty statistics. Officers who fought under Shelby "rode in the vanguard, not in some pantywaist rear-rank echelon as some did!" Ryerson had often loudly proclaimed in recalling his service under the Secessionist flag.

Spunky shook his head imperceptibly. Four years under Jo Shelby and twenty years of frontier law-keeping equipped Ryerson to track men of bad dispositions as well as to lead men of stout heart—a single companion or a squad-size patrol such as this *posse comitatus* of Ryerson's old trail pards.

True to Ryerson's and Donovan's strategic plan, the two packhorse managers and the two point riders were staggered in a column of twos and two horselengths apart.

"You're doin' fine! Keep Regulation Number Two well in mind. Spread out, column of twos, far apart across the road, a horse or two length between," Ryerson's hoarse voice called out once they were well out of town. "If Ike shoots into a mob of bunched-up riders, he's bound to unhorse one, maybe two. Spread out, they don't know who to take a sight on, and even if they do, those gimp-eyed jaspers will likely miss. We'll be alerted and be on 'em like riled-up hornets!"

The sun that had finally pushed away the gray dews and damps of morning and then rained down fire on them most of the day let itself gradually down behind a rolling low range to the west when Ryerson called a final halt. As it did, the land turned pleasantly balmy. The day had passed without a sign of hide nor hair of Ike's gang.

"I'm just as relieved," Ryerson said, flinging a stirrup over the saddle and loosening Jo Shelby's cinch. "You can be sure Bodene has scouts out and has gotten wind of us by now."

Spunky Smith, unsaddling Old Stockholder close to Cap Donovan, caught Cap's gaze. The aging lawman's eyebrows arched in recognition of Cole's words, his eyes glittering in anticipation at Spunky. Spunky winked at old Cap; this was going to be a ride to end all rides.

After a day in the saddle, Ryerson's Renegades, as Cactus Jack had dubbed them when he and Spunky sat down together in the middle of the afternoon to work out the saddle kinks and have a smoke, were within eight miles of the trail crossing of the Southern and Central line near where the outlaw bunch had pulled off the express car robbery.

The posse men had stripped off their saddles and rubbed down all their animals, including the pack-horses and replacements, with small gunnysacks Ryerson and Maguire had provided for in the gear on the packhorses. They led their remuda down to a nearby stream for water. Under Fernando's keen-eyed supervision from horseback, the horses were allowed to graze for an hour before being tied to a picket line strung between two big rocks.

Others were busy organizing the gear for night camp. Spunky worked alongside Cap Donovan, who allowed as to how he was so hungry his belly had shrunk down so it "wouldn't so much as chamber a Meskin bean." A pleasant feel came over the bunch as daylight waned and a draft of cool air drifted through their camp.

Ryerson, coming back from checking Jo Shelby, found his five cronies with the camp chores about done, ready to relax after a day in the saddle.

"Well, sir," Ryerson said, surveying the operation with his eyebrow cocked. "I suppose I'd say this here first night's camp is in shipshape, apple-pie order. A good omen for the morrow."

"Many hands make light work," Seabring said happily.

"Depends on the number of men all trying to light the lamp at once, perfesser," Ryerson quipped, watching for their response. Some of them got it; some didn't. He turned serious. "We'll start a supper fire in about twenty minutes. I'll take charge of heating up some beans and fry up some bacon. I'll whomp up some bread dough and you all can wrap it on a stick to bake over the fire. The bacon grease'll be a good flavoring when your bread's done."

There were murmurs of agreement and enthusiasm among the men clustered around Ryerson. Despite their meager rations, five mouths collectively began to water. It had been that kind of first day.

Cap figured there was a possibility of fleshing out the menu. "If it's all the same to you, Cole," he said, "I believe I'll also ride out and see what game's in these parts."

"Capital idea, Captain!" Ryerson enthused. "You do as you're of a mind. Watch for ambush. But don't rush off. There's still considerable of twilight left. I figure before we eat, we should set about salutin' our first day in the saddle with a dollop or two of old Bravemaker. Your cups, gentlemen?"

Spunky dug in his mess gear for his tin cup and was one of the first back to Ryerson, who struggled with awkward fingers to persuade a tightly fitted cob out of a huge crockery jug; it exited with a resounding "thung," and Ryerson hoisted the jug to splash a goodly quantity into Spunky's vessel.

Without waiting for the others for some kind of toast, as if waiting was expected of him, Spunky raised the rim to his lips for a pleasing, if tentative, sip. When a packhorse lugged it at great effort all the way out here and in homage to the peaceful, God-built surroundings, a man who took pleasure in his drinking didn't just swill down his hootch like a hog at the trough. He went about it gently, respectfully, savoring the gentility of its mood-altering mellowness.

Through the whiskey's bite, Spunky could feel the day's accumulation of trail dust that had coated the roof of his mouth and his throat being physically scoured away by the potent brew. Its biting taste or aroma, or a combination of the two, also permeated upward, its potent tang clearing his breathing passages, similarly alkali-clogged.

"'y damn!" he gasped. "That there'll put hair on your chest!"

"And maybe start some sprouts on your shoulder blades," Ryerson allowed. The marshal hooked the jug handle on his index finger, supporting and raising the massive, heavy crock with his elbow, the neck in a direct line with his eager, uptilted mouth. Spunky watched in amazement and admiration as Ryerson's Adam's apple bobbed with three giant swigs. Ryerson dropped the jug off his arm and back to the ground with a resounding thunk. "Paaah!" he groaned, smacking his lips. "Spunky, I can feel *that* starting whiskers where I sit my horse! Whoo!"

"You think we'll cut old Ike's trail come mornin', Cole?"

"Who's to know, Spunky," Ryerson said, turning serious. "Tomorrow or the next. We got to find him by the third day. And we will."

Hans Seabring appeared and almost timidly thrust out his cup. Ryerson willingly obliged. "When the whiskey's nearly gone, perfesser, we'll dispatch Cactus Jack to town for reinforcements and a night under Bertha's canopy to recruit his native strengths and talents. Never let it be said Cole Ryerson did not look after the welfare of his men. Your health, Doctor," he said, balancing the jug again on his elbow.

"If you're so all-fired concerned about our well-being," Spunky admonished, "then why in hell didn't you cart along some of those loose women from town?"

Ryerson didn't miss a beat. "Dissipation, my dear Spunky. Dissipation! I need stouthearted men on this cotillion, not men ground down by the evil lusts of the flesh. John Barleycorn is a right proper companion for the trail, so long as he is appropriately and temperately administered. I hold in the vilest contempt that man who allows alcohol to make a fool and an idiot of himself. And do you honestly think dragging along women—women of casual virtue and temperament to boot—would do anything but tear this *posse comitatus* to shreds?"

Spunky had endured Ryerson's soliloquy wide-eyed in rapt attention. It seemed that the older "Boot Hill Cole" got the more long-winded he became.

Near them, Dr. Seabring, unperturbed by Ryerson's recitation, held his filled cup inches from his nose. Like the true scientist he was, with cupped hand and fingers he beckoned a whiff of the bourbon's aroma toward his nose. Satisfied that the elixir was sufficiently toxic, the astronomer took a robust swig. "And to yours, Cole," he said, bringing the cup away from his mouth. "And to your health, Mr. Smith."

Spunky and Cole stared at the astronomer bemused. Then the light dawned. Moments before his temperance lecture began, Ryerson had toasted the good doctor's health.

"Spunky, Herr Perfesser. Not Mr. Smith," Ryerson declared.

"Spunky," Seabring responded, relaxing his natural reserve.

"Thanks, Doc," Spunky said, being a man of few words.

"How'd he come by the name Spunky?" Seabring asked.

Ryerson grinned. "Well, Spunky?"

Spunky felt the burning of blush flooding his cheeks. "Aw, I dunno. It was just about always there, I reckon." He hoped Ryerson could leave it at that.

"Come on, Spunky," Ryerson teased.

"Spunky's good enough!"

"Not good enough," Ryerson persisted. "Are you a

real man, one who owns up to the truth, or it is that you ain't really worth riding with this posse?"

Spunky glared at Ryerson; he sure could get a man's goat. For a moment, Spunky hated Cole Ryerson and his pesky ways. He decided to let it ride and just clam up.

"Well?" Ryerson taunted, an annoying, tormenting tone still there.

As he always did when he was pushed or somebody prodded a friend, Spunky saw red. "Hahdammit, Cole, you're so mouthy and so know-it-all this evenin', you tell 'im. Judas! I don't know why I ever agreed to ride over here and help you!"

"I tell you, Doc," Ryerson said, turning talkative with his quantity of Old Group Tightener. "Spunky's a man to make a camp with. Got a fuse on him about as short-gaited as he is. But when the chips are down—buffalo or poker—you'll not find a stouter *compañero* backin' your play or sharin' your camp!"

Ryerson was silent a long time, his eyes distant. "Many's the night," he said finally, "I've charged into a San Patricio fleshpot to face a drunk or quell a fracas and had Spunky's hind end rubbing mine, watching my back trail. I'll never want for a stouter man to protect my blind side than Spunky Smith."

For a moment, Spunky basked in the glory of Ryerson's words, but an evil glint of eye said Ryerson wasn't through ragging him. "Tell Doc about bein' spunky, Spunky!"

Spunky glared at Ryerson. "I should've let the hahdam Pruitt boys take you that night!"

"That was it!" Ryerson cheered, remembering. "That night in San Patrice Spunky and I'd seen to it that the Pruitt boys' baby brother was behind bars, ready for trial. He'd murdered, and hangin' was too good for the little snot.

"I wasn't expectin' trouble. Leon and Dale Pruitt was and got the drop on me. I couldn't draw or they'd've dusted me in a wink and taken the key and turned their kid brother loose."

Ryerson looked at Spunky, who saw great admiration in the marshal's respectful eyes, and his smoldering temper lost its edge like a sharp knife trying to cut a rock.

"First thing I know, Spunky was beside me, his Colt out at the hip. 'Boys,' he says, 'let's let the marshal unlimber his big iron. We'll all shoot when the barkeep drops a hat and see who's left standin'!' I tell you, Doc, them Pruitts lowered their antlers, sleeved their plowhandle Colts, and slunk on out of there like whipped dogs. We hanged Donny Pruitt in the mornin' on schedule. Leon and Dale didn't show up till the next day to claim the remains. Even then sheepish as hell.

"An old saloon whore allowed as to how what Deputy Sylvester Smith done was pretty spunky, and Spunky he's been ever since!"

"Amazing!" Seabring said. "Nothing short of amazing!"

"Hush!" Ryerson hissed in an alarmed whisper. "What the hell's that noise?" His body tensed, and his chin lifted as he pivoted, ears searching for an as yet unclear sound.

An uneven rumbling sound, softened by considerable distance, grew, and with it a raucous jangle and chatter were transported on the air. The posse men dropped what they were doing, put down cups, tools, or leathers and harkened with eyes averted to concentrate fully on identifying the approaching sound.

"See to your sidearms!" Ryerson commanded with a hiss. "Lever a round into your Winchesters, relax the hammers, mind your muzzles, and look to secure cover. Paint for war!"

The mysterious sound grew closer and louder, its bouncing cacophony chopping away the desert's deathly silence like a battery of dull axes. Spunky hunkered tensely behind a hummock of gravel while Fernando, Cap, and Cactus Jack deployed themselves at random distances down a narrow, trenchlike wash. Ryerson and Seabring peered anxiously around either side of an enormous and pocked tawny granite boulder that over eons had rolled its way down, around, and across the desert landscape to serve as protection for just this moment.

Gray-barreled Winchesters and Seabring's big handsome Sharps with its lustrous, case-hardened receiver, all up and at the ready, poked gun muzzles out like a family of water moccasins on a calm creek.

Over a soft sloping ridge from the direction the posse had come, a team of horse heads emerged, taking full form and plodding down the trail dragging a small buckboard whose diminutive driver wore a hat with a tall crown like an upended deep bowl, its broad brim turned down all around. The driver had on a tan canvas trail coat with a deeper, dun-colored corduroy collar buttoned closely at the throat, more to keep out the dust than for warmth.

Near him, Spunky heard Cactus Jack mutter, "I don't believe it!" Ryerson's deputy recklessly pulled himself out of his hiding place in the wash.

On the other side of him, Spunky saw Ryerson rise stiff and red-faced in impatience. "Mr. Maguire! Front and center!" Cactus Jack loped self-consciously up to him and stood at a civilian's interpretation of attention.

"Jack! What in the Lord's name is *this* all about?!"

"I'm in the dark same as you, Cole," Maguire murmured almost apologetically.

"You better be!" Ryerson roared. "It's all right, gentlemen!" he called. "You can come out of your holes now." Then more softly, but still raucously insistent. "Jack, what in the hell is your wife doing way out here!?"

"I don't know anything about this, Cole," Maguire said, fawning. "Maybe something happened in town." Without waiting for concurrence, Maguire set his rifle aside and loped to the approaching buckboard, its jostling racket quieting as the driver slowed the two-horse team. The others found safe places for their loaded rifles and gathered close to a glowering Ryerson as he watched Maguire go.

Mrs. Maguire halted the team and buckboard, wrapped the reins around the whip socket, climbed down, and lustily embraced and kissed her bewildered husband.

His cheeks red as summer berries, Cactus Jack sent an imploring look back at his fellow posse men, clustered some distance away. He murmured an unheard question of his spouse, got the reply, and

Spunky distinctly heard him exclaim, "Well, Bertha, what did you do that for?"

To Spunky, Mrs. Maguire looked different in trail clothes than she had the night before when, in the flowing, voluminous frock of a proper hostess, she spread the festive board in her home for Ryerson's Renegades. Spunky had been duly respectful but had otherwise paid Bertha Maguire's physical attributes little mind.

Spunky now perceived that Bertha was chunky-built, bosomy, with the stout neck and wrists of a woman who would be a tireless, fastidious housekeeper and equally durable and altogether sporty between the sheets.

"All right, Bertha," Spunky heard Cactus Jack remark loudly, "but you tell 'im." The two of them marched toward the puzzled knot of posse men, their attention directed at Cole Ryerson.

Though he was astonished and angered, Ryerson didn't forget his manners. "Mrs. Maguire," he said, respectfully. "Good evenin' to you, ma'am."

"Mr. Ryerson," Bertha responded sweetly. "A pleasure to see you." Spunky noted that her eyes, a fetching shade of green, had that same strong, unflinching quality as Ryerson's—a glint of determination that said you'd better listen and heed.

As leader of the group, Ryerson naturally took the lead. "May I inquire the nature of your visit, Mrs. Maguire?" Still the tone of his voice registered bewilderment. Others crowded around, mouths agape, eyes big as bowls, and minds abuzz with the same question.

Bertha Maguire's response was firm, yet tender. "You men have had a tedious, tiring first day on the trail. I know how important this mission is to all of you, Mr. Ryerson." Still, a snippy tone emerged in her words; Spunky forgave her for as Ryerson had explained, she was a very thorough woman. "After I got John's things ready this morning and fed him"—and Spunky could see Cactus Jack's expression becoming more bashful—"I thought how nice it would be if you men had a hot, home-cooked meal your first night out!"

"That's why you're here, Bertha?" Ryerson asked, incredulous. "You came all the way out here, nearly thirty miles? To feed us?"

"I got my windows washed while the hens were cooking," she declared matter-of-factly. "I've fixed a generous portion of chicken and dumplings for all of you with some potatoes and cooked vegetables and Grandmother Riehl's nice porcelain tureen full of thick giblet gravy."

Six mouths drooled; Spunky swallowed hard to keep from having to spit.

"If you'll see to getting a fire going, Mr. Ryerson," she said, "and if some of your men will help Mr. Maguire and me unload those boxes someplace handy and somebody look to the care of my team, I'll get busy and get things warmed over in a jiffy."

Ryerson looked around at the men, his expression revealing the embarrassing fact that they were totally and irreversibly stumped. "Fernando! Spunky! Roust yourselves and help the lady unload!"

Now that explanations were dispensed with, Bertha Maguire took charge. "You men go off somewhere with your whiskey . . . Oh, don't fret, Mr. Ryerson. This is your territory, not mine. You needn't worry about my feelings. In my home, it's different. You all clean up after you've done your precious drinking and had your man talk, and I'll have a nice hot meal set for you in about three quarters of an hour."

3

When he'd helped Bertha Maguire get herself geared up to fix supper, Spunky parked his Winchester against the same rock where he'd left his still half-filled cup of whiskey. He trotted his cup over to Ryerson, and the others hunkered in a rude circle like a covey of quail in the draw, their conversation a muted dull monotone as he approached. Cactus Jack, ever the devoted husband, and the gracious, obedient Fernando, stayed behind with Bertha to run whatever little errands came to her mind as she skittered about warming the grand supper she had prepared.

Crouched closest to Ryerson, Cap Donovan was hatless, his fine white hair whipping in the late afternoon breeze like cottonwood fuzz. While Spunky squatted in a gap between Cap and Dr. Seabring and nursed his whiskey, the rest marveled at the domestic phenomenon they witnessed.

"How in the everlasting hell did she do it, Cole?"

Cap asked. "We rode steady all day, stopping only a couple of times for brief relief. And here's a woman bustles around—after we ride out—cooks chickens and all the trimmin's, washes all her windows, harnesses the team, loads up and heads out, gettin' here not twenty minutes behind us. How in hell did she manage it!?"

Cole Ryerson's expression was bewildered as he watched through the dwindling twilight at Bertha skittering like one of her hens between the fire and her wagon, quietly but firmly giving orders to her two kitchen helpers, Fernando and Cactus Jack, meekly doing what they were told.

Ryerson had only one response. "Mrs. Maguire is a very thorough woman," he repeated dryly, his cocked eye following the competent little creature as she went about her chores.

"Chicken, dumplings, and all the groceries and giblet gravy to match to feed this small army," Spunky enthused. "If she weren't a frail lady, I sure wouldn't mind to have her along on the trail if her grub's always that good!"

"Judas! Don't let her hear you say that!" Ryerson cautioned. "If she gets that idea into her head, there'll be no escape for us. And hell to pay. We don't need a problem like that on our hands."

"We could all take a lesson from this," Hans Seabring cut in with a schoolteacher tone.

"Which is?" Ryerson eyed his scientist friend suspiciously.

"Planning, Cole, planning. That is how she does it. Thinking ahead. Organizing your work, setting small goals which together achieve the larger goal. Contemplate each step, and weigh the alternatives of each. That's her secret. Organization."

Ryerson squinted quizzically at Dr. Seabring, his ruffled feelings evident. "You trying to tell me, perfesser, that I haven't calculated every move, anticipated each contingency on this here *soiree?*"

"Perish the thought, Cole. We're well equipped and geared for our quest. No one is ever so perfect, though, that he cannot benefit from observing the keys to the success of another."

Ryerson released a grunt that resembled a sinister belch. "Humph! You're right, perfesser. A very thorough person indeed. The subject of thoroughness reminds me that we ain't put out any sentries. Too much preoccupied with meaningless camp chores and the invasion of that woman in spite of her grand supper, and getting our spirits bracketed better with some of this nose paint. Ike Bodene is a past master at stealing your horses, your women, or your scalp before you know he's in camp. This here palaver about Mrs. Maguire and her thorough ways prompts me to suggest that you, Cap, and Spunky take your rifles and patrol opposite circles around our perimeter."

Spunky spoke up, pleading, upset that Seabring had to go and open his big yap and fill Ryerson's head with such notions at the wrong time. "But, Cole, she's about to ring the supper bell." Cap Donovan also gave Ryerson a distressful frown. Neither of their reactions was missed by Cole Ryerson.

"Now don't you fellows fret. Soon's me and Hans here have our grub, we'll grab our rifles and come up and relieve you. There's gonna be plenty of chuck to go around and then some, if I know little Mrs. Maguire, even if all of us just now's got a hollow cavity down there like a bear fresh from hibernatin'.' "

Cap and Spunky wrinkled their foreheads at each other, gulped down the dregs in their whiskey cups, and rose up stiffly to see to their rifles.

"I reckon it'll taste better if we have to wait a while," Spunky muttered to Cap as the two of them slouched out of the wash bed.

"Leave it to you to find the silver lining, Spunky," Cap said. "You circle clockwise and I'll go counter." Cap found his Winchester in the gathering dark and, levering down the breech, confirmed a live round. "Maintain about fifty yards from the fire and we'll be bound to meet each other twice in the circle and not shoot anybody by mistake."

"Lonelier, but better'n walking together, and that's a fact," Spunky said. "Makes a great deal less of a target for some of Bad-Face Ike's dry-gulchers."

"And more effective perimeter coverage," Cap declared. "As Dr. Seabring says, we got to become very thorough people—like Mrs. Maguire."

Spunky thought about that one; even with the deadly threat of the Bodene gang, he didn't know if it was necessary for them to become quite as agonizingly thorough as Bertha Maguire. She was a package for a man of his experience to behold.

Fifty yards or so out into the deepening night, away from the fire's glow, the two sentinels separated.

"See you across from camp," Cap called softly in the night.

"When I hear you coming, I'll whistle like a bird, Cap."

"I'll do the same," Cap said, his words disappearing with his form into the dark. "'Ceptin' I can't whistle worth a hoot."

"Then hoot," Spunky quipped.

As Spunky strolled on his patrol, his boots crunching in the gravel, night fell around him, dark as the inside of a bedroll. A star or two ventured into the soft, inky dome above him, summoning others that soon would fill the awesome overhead depths like tiny diamonds displayed upon black velvet.

Below him, in the tawny and tiny bowl of desert, Cactus Jack clanged an iron-rod triangle his wife had hauled along, calling Ryerson and Seabring to supper. Spunky's stomach growled at the thought of hot chicken and dumplings, smothered with a heaping ladle of soul-satisfying giblet gravy.

Spunky's route took him behind a tall, rounded hummock of broken-down granite studded with boulders and stubby clumps of powder gray sage. In the darkness, totally shielded from the comforting light of the supper fire, Spunky's senses turned alert to any sounds uncommon to the desert stillness. He trod softly, reluctant to deprive his ears of any sounds that might signal danger.

When he rounded the sloping far side of the hummock where it merged with the desert flats, he hungrily studied the movement of figures illuminated in the fire's light as they crouched with their plates and enthused over the quality and quantity of Mrs. Maguire's chuck. Now and again they went back to the chicken pot warming by the fire for second helpings or carefully lifted the lid of Bertha's grandmother's precious porcelain tureen for more giblet gravy.

Dammit, Cole, he thought, get busy and feed your damned tapeworm and get on up here so I can go eat! It almost seemed as though Cole was taking his own dear, sweet time just to spite Spunky.

He tensed with a muffled hoot from out of the night ahead of him; he bird-whistled his response. "That you, Cap?" he called guardedly.

"Ain't Bad-Face Ike," Cap called, his form taking shape out of the dark ahead. Cap sounded perturbed. "Had it've been, I'd've had a knife between your ribs and your scalp on my shirt by now. You stomp the ground with all the grace of a Missouri mule and just about as wide awake!"

Spunky bristled with resentment. "I just wondered when them two down there was going to get their plates sopped up and come on up here and let us go down and eat."

"Tighten your belt, son, and forget it," Cap advised. "Your mind needs to be up here, not down there. All quiet in your sector?"

"As a tomb. How about you?"

"Me and a jackrabbit gave one another a start back a ways. When he figured a hasty retreat preferable to confrontation, I dogged nigh hammered back Old Oliver here." Cap gestured with his Winchester. "But when I'm on guard, I always make certain to know the cause of the commotion before I start shootin'."

"Good thinking," Spunky said.

"Beats wastin' ca'tridges and maybe shootin' your pard. Well, see you on the other side of the bowl, Spunky."

"Wisht it was over the gravy bowl."

"There you go again, son. Get your mind off your gut and don't keep studyin' the damned camp," Cap called gruffly over his shoulder, his form again losing its shape in the dark. Spunky started off on his rounds; Cap's voice followed him. "Attack's going to come from the other way, son. That's where you got to watch. And mind you let your feet down light."

Spunky figured he'd let that be the last of the palaver for now. Every outfit, he mused, still sensing an uncomfortable bristling inside him, has got to have its gawdam experts.

Nonetheless, he found his eyes probing the darkness of the desert outside his patrol perimeter and staying aware of the softness of his footfalls. Cap, he mused—at last turning philosophical—might be an old fussbudget and rankle a man at times, but he made practical sense.

Spunky tried to forget his nagging stomach and the best way, he discovered, was—as Cap had advised—to ignore the supper firelight.

Once, when he did sneak a glance campward, he saw figures he took to be Cactus Jack and Fernando pick up their rifles and stride off into the dark. Cactus Jack appeared to be headed his way, but on an angle that would cross Spunky's patrol line well ahead of him.

Spunky walked faster in hopes of more quickly intercepting young Maguire. He had walked through the dense desert night but a few minutes when he became aware of footsteps in the distance. He called out in a hushed tone, "Maguire?"

"Yeah. That you, Cap?"

"Huh-uh. What if I was to say it was Ike Bodene? No, it's me. Spunky."

"You sure walk soft, Mr. Smith. Boy, you'd've snuck up on me easy." Spunky glowed; he'd get Maguire somehow to tell that to Cap when they all got back to camp. "Cole says I'm to be your relief," Cactus Jack continued, his voice looming larger as he approached Spunky in the night. "You're to go down and get fed."

"Music to my ears," Spunky emoted as the two grew close enough to recognize each other in the dark. "I thought Cole and Doc Seabring was coming to relieve us."

Maguire chuckled. "I offered. Told Cole I'd appreciate havin' a chance to stretch my legs."

Spunky grinned in the dark. "Sounds like that weren't the truth."

"I had enough of being the camp kicker for today," Jack confessed. "Fernando was savvy enough to see what I was getting at and told Cole he wanted to walk off his supper, too. I reminded Cole how much he hates walkin' these days and suddenly found myself on my way out of camp for a change." Rejoicing rang in Cactus Jack's voice.

A relieved Spunky felt his stomach grumbling agreeably.

"Soon as you fellas eat," Jack continued, "Bertha's going to appoint volunteers to help with the dishes, and it won't be you or Cap—particularly if you dawdle over your grub. Word to the wise, you might say, Spunky. I'd be *numero uno* on her list. Now it's

Cole Ryerson. And I figure Doc Seabring's had a lot of practice washing laboratory bottles and such. Bertha will think of that, too."

"You got a lot of mischief in you, Cactus Jack."

"Not mischief really, Spunky. Bertha attends to everything at home pretty well and figures my job is to bring home the bacon and beans. At that, she manages to find enough for me to do around the place. A man quick ciphers out ways around that without riling things in the nest.

"I don't see nothing devious in that. A man sometimes does what he has to do."

"You got your makin's, Spunky?"

Spunky fished in his vest and handed over his Bull Durham sack. "Lightin' a match or walkin' an inch or two behind a little ember like that makes a man a prime target in the night, Jack."

"I ain't going to have but the one, Spunky. Belly's full, it's a fine night, and a smoke's just about all a man needs."

Spunky figured with a young wife out there in that same fine night, Cactus Jack would be getting something else he needed that the others would be deprived of. But he figured not to bring it up. He also knew it wasn't healthy for a man in his situation just now to ponder such thoughts too deeply.

"Walk soft and keep your eyes away from the campfire and out into the desert where the danger's likely to come from," Spunky advised, almost quoting Cap Donovan word for word.

"Good advice. You're a first-class lawman and tracker, and that's a fact. A man like me can learn a lot from you."

Spunky glowed a little and decided to continue the lesson. "And be aware where your partner is at all times. No need to waste ca'tridges or maybe shoot the other fella out here with you."

"Don't fret, Spunky. I'll heed your warning."

"And it's a good idea to walk as soft as you can. Lay your feet down easy."

"Sure easy to see how you came through all these years with your scalp."

"Just makes good sense, that's all," he tossed back at Cactus Jack as he brought his Winchester to a carefree shoulder arms and began a fast walk in the direction of the campfire.

Cap was in camp well ahead of him and had loaded a plate with chicken, dumplings, and boiled spuds. As Spunky walked up, Cap hovered over the enormous thick white-and-blue-figured porcelain tureen ladling hot, thick, creamy giblet gravy over his heap of steaming grub. Mrs. Maguire watched Cap with pride and satisfaction as she poured Cap's coffee from a huge enameled pot close to the fire.

The smell of mesquite smoke blending with cooked chicken and coffee turned Spunky's salivary glands into regular artesian wells.

"You're the last to be fed, Mr. Smith," Bertha proclaimed as Spunky grabbed a plate and headed for the iron pot where the chicken and dumplings and potatoes stayed warm close to the fire. "Mr. Donovan couldn't get another teaspoonful on his plate if he tried, and there's plenty left for you."

Bertha Maguire still wore her trail coat and slouch felt hat, which looked oddly out of place with the starched and frilly cotton calico-print apron over the front of her.

"I'll be beholden, Mr. Smith," she continued, "if you can scrape and spoon my pots and my tureen clean with your portion. I like to see a man eat, and I purely despise throwing good food out for the bugs and the varmints."

Spunky grinned with a sublime gratitude at Mrs. Maguire and said nothing as he went about filling his plate. There were advantages, he suddenly realized, in being the last one in the grub line.

Spunky crouched close to the fire and spooned and forked in his supper like a starving wolf, his admiring eyes following Bertha as she busied herself with cleaning and organizing her pots and utensils after the meal.

"Mr. Ryerson and Dr. Seabring," she announced in a tone that suggested she'd brook no disobedience. "You'll do me the honor of heating some water and shaving some soap for my dishes. And warm some rinse water. There are a couple of dish towels in my box in the buckboard. You'll need them, too."

Spunky grinned inwardly; Cactus Jack was right about her.

Ryerson's face said he was about to object on the grounds that he was the leader of the expedition. The next second, his expression told Spunky that he'd thought better of it. Yes, she was a very thorough woman.

"Oh, I know Mr. Maguire insisted on going out as guard to get out of his chores," she continued.

"It's all right, Bertha," Ryerson reassured her. "I reckon I'd druther play pearl diver anyway. Walkin' and I ain't on the best of terms." Ryerson and Seabring eased out of their places by the fire and headed for the Maguire buckboard.

"Oh, Mr. Ryerson," she called after them. "In the same box with the soap and my dish towels, you'll find three nice apple pies. I didn't tell my will-o'-the-wisp husband. It'll serve him right. There's a half a pie for each of you men. Including Mr. Maguire when he comes in, of course. I baked them last evening after the mister went to bed."

Ecstatic with the thought of having a whole half a fresh apple pie all to himself, holding his plate Spunky roused up, and went to clean out the chicken pot and the gravy tureen as he'd been bid by Mrs. Maguire. He heard Cap Donovan shatter the air with a gratified belch.

"And those aren't your second-rate dried apple pies either, Mr. Ryerson," she called after her two helpers. "Those are from fresh Winesaps of Mrs. Sherman, my dear lady friend in Fort Walker. Her mister brought the cuttings all the way out from Ohio with them. They were full-grown bearing trees before her mister was called to the Lord two years ago."

Ryerson and Dr. Seabring returned to the fire with Ryerson juggling wash pots and soap and towels, while the scientist deftly managed three full pie tins. Each plate-sized narrow-rimmed tin was filled with rounded, flaky, and ornately scored crusts, all richly but lightly browned and glowing with the glaze of a light sugared coating. The sculptured crust rims were handsomely pinched and puckered. Spunky tried hard to remember when camp grub had been so good. He couldn't.

"Put the wash things over there, Mr. Ryerson," she ordered. "By the way, when you assign your guard schedule for the night, you may leave Mr. Maguire's name off. We will make our bed some distance from camp, and he'll be properly occupied with his domestic responsibilities till in the morning."

Taken aback by Mrs. Maguire's candor, a startled Spunky glanced Ryerson's way to see the marshal's eyes wide in unabashed astonishment.

Ryerson watched the receding figures of Cactus Jack and Bertha Maguire disappear out of the firelight toward their remote bedroll-for-two.

With other posse men sitting, crouching, or squatting around the fire, some thoughtfully nursing prebedtime cigarettes, Ryerson grabbed his cup and hunted up the whiskey jug. With a robust cupful, he trudged back. He took a healthy sip as he hunkered down near the blaze, holding the cup in both hands. He stared into the fire in an absorbed, distant way for a long moment. The others watched him expectantly.

"I don't know about you fellas," he said finally, "but with the kind of a day it's been, I need what you might call a nightcap. If any of you care to join me, help yourselves." He offered the jug, and it began to make the rounds.

After his moments of quiet reflection at the fireside, Ryerson seemed inclined to chat.

"Dr. Seabring yonder, now, he'd probably prefer to uncover his telescope and commence studying the stars. Guess I haven't properly explained to you gents the presence of Dr. Hans Seabring with our *posse comitatus.*"

Spunky looked over at the scientist squatted by the fire. He was a spare, dried-up looking man with blond hair bleaching with age, and beady, curious eyes. His complexion, Spunky noted earlier in the day, said he was usually stranger to the sun.

To shield himself from that sun, Seabring wore a broad brimmed, flat-crowned, off-white, thin straw hat with a narrow black-ribboned hatband. His slender form was cloaked in a similarly colored linen coat associated with those of scientific mien. His gleaming, foxlike eyes rested above oval lens eyeglasses with a spring-loaded bridge clamped to his nose. Another thin black ribbon dangled to his coat lapel in case something happened to jar loose his looking-glasses.

Spunky could never remember if they were called pince-nez or Nez Percé glasses. Seabring wore a carefully trimmed Vandyke-style beard, uncommon on the frontier where most men were clean shaved to prevent vermin infestation.

"Gentlemen," Ryerson went on. "In this fracas, while we are all snuggled warm and safe in our tarps and soogans, Herr Perfesser Seabring will likely be out amongst the coyotes and the chaparral on the nearest promontory fixing his all-knowing eye upon the heavens, looking for more planets. Right, Hans?"

"It's *hahntz,* my dear Ryerson," he corrected. "Not *huntss.* You say it always wrong. I correct you and next time you say again *huntss!*" Then Seabring's troubled frown relaxed, his eyes taking on an almost angelic softness as he rolled them toward the silent, star-studded black inverted dome over him.

Ryerson took a sip of his neck oil, studying the scientist who stood up like a classroom lecturer, eyes upon the heavens, one hand casually clutching his lapel.

"But only one planet really, Cole. I knew where the others are. Don't have to search. We of the science of astronomy—or should I say a small group of my colleagues, myself included—theorize the existence of a ninth planet at the outer reaches of the solar system somewhere inside or outside the orbit of Neptune. I am determined to be the first to discover and thus confirm it. The clear, open skies of the West are particularly conducive to such telescopic observations."

Spunky understood part—but not all—of the astronomer's palaver. Ryerson was in the same boat, for he interrupted.

"Lest I tread upon your scientific sentence, Herr Perfesser, I want to set at ease any qualms my associates here have of nursemaiding a man of scientific cloth while we face the hazards of running to earth that squaw-mounting derelict Ike Bodene. Sit down, Doctor. You may treat us to your lectures on the marvels of Saturn and Venus when we are bored to tears of evenings and have stomached enough of this coffin varnish to tolerate heavy doses of your astronomical drivel."

Ryerson was at it again, Spunky thought. Sometimes it was hard to tell when callous wisecracks departed from true feelings.

Not altogether comprehending, Dr. Seabring crouched again by the fire, first flipping back his duster's tails so as not to unduly wrinkle them.

Ryerson still wasn't through with him. "Don't think

for a minute, gents, that Dr. Honce Seabring is not worth his salt. He retained me in what, Doctor? Eighteen and seventy-five? I guided him on a mission of scientific inquiry among the glorious peaks of northern New Mexico. Let me add here that Herr Perfesser Seabring—as you all saw this afternoon—packs a beautifully mounted Sharps action .45/70 rifle in the same thick leathern tube that supports and protects his scientific telescope."

Ryerson walked close to where Seabring sat and fondly rested a hand on the scientist's shoulder; as Seabring looked up at Ryerson, the tiny glass ovals flanking his nose became brilliant mirrors of the flickering firelight.

"One afternoon in camp, while I enjoyed a few swigs of old Group Tightener and Dr. Seabring held forth with the glories of the physical universe, a crowd of throat-cutting, scalp-lifting Comanches that infest that territory snuck up on us and commenced sendin' a hail of flint arrows and lead our way.

"Aware that discretion is often the better part of valor, I discreetly shot our two mounts and the packhorses in a circle of breastworks around a buffalo wallow. It was a protective little basin with a quantity of seepage into which the great American bison had pissed and otherwise relieved himself. In the extreme, at least it offered water supply. Dr. Seabring and I painted for war ourselves and proceeded to hold those hell-screamin' Comanches at arm's length for the balance of the evenin'.

"In the dark, and me not convinced the Comanches mightn't mount a stealth attack by night, Dr. Seabring managed to set up his telescope within the confines of our by now rather whiffy little fort and continued to record the results of his asternomical observations."

Seabring's voice interrupted. "It was scientifically incumbent upon me to continue to gather my data unperturbed." Again Spunky struggled with the scientist's words.

"Come daylight," Ryerson went on, "cool as a Ute Indian with a contented squaw, Dr. Seabring locked his telescope down horizontal upon the Comanches ringing us roundabout. He sighted in his magic eye and his Sharps on the chief of the war party. They was off there six, seven hundred yards if they was an inch, and through that telescope, I swear I could've counted the notches on that old bastard's coup stick!

"I watched through the eyepiece as Doc's first round cuffed the dust twenty feet in front of the old chief who stood there brazen as a brass monkey, persuaded of his invincibility at the range. I suggested that Doc raise his muzzle a couple of degrees, which, bein' a scientist, he understood most admirably and which he did with most uncommon pluck. Doc's second shot was dead-on, excuse the expression, penetratin' the chief's bone hare-pipe breastplate, passin' clean through to knock over dead as a doornail the medicine man standin' smack-dab behind him! That took the starch out of them Comanches, I'm here to tell you. Along about then, they packed their war bags and went home, haulin' their dead with em.

"They was awed, no other word for it. And they didn't pester me and Hans any more that trip. That night we was so at ease that we watched a star occupation of Saturn through the telescope, wasn't that it, Hans?"

"Close," Seabring said, grinning with patience and acceptance of Ryerson and his fumbling ways. "Actually a stellar occultation, Cole. A star passing behind Saturn—a most significant phenomenon, duly recorded in my journal."

Again, it was Ryerson's turn. "Gents—and mark well my words—the only time Doc Seabring'll whimper is if it looks like some mishap might befall his telescope." He paused, studying the firelit scientist with great admiration. "Apart from that, this here scientific jasper is all horns and rattles . . . clear to the bone!"

4

Dawn was scarcely a reality when Cactus Jack limped unsteadily to the morning fire looking like a horse that had been rode hard and put away wet, but with a sheepish grin a mile wide.

The others crouched close to the blaze to absorb what warmth they could while warming their insides with coffee near too thick to drink and barely too thin to plow. Cactus Jack's saddle mates studied him with glances just a shade away from a glare; there was little mystery how he'd spent the night, and their envy was close to the surface.

Maguire gaped and stretched languidly and let out a long sigh before folding down to a vacant spot close to the fire, snagging a clean cup and filling it.

"Go ahead, Jack," Ryerson said, condescendingly. "Appears you'll require a share of reconstitutin' this mornin'." Jack seemed to take no umbrage at Cole's insinuations. The others stared longingly or wistfully at young Maguire, remembering some of their own unforgettable and similar mornings after.

Cactus Jack, his cheeks aflush with gratification and good humor, slurped in a magnificent sip of the hearty brew oblivious, it seemed to Spunky, to its lip- and tongue-blistering fierceness.

"It's a gorgeous mornin', ain't it," Cactus Jack enthused. The others, regarding the chill and murkiness of dawn, disagreed but still murmured a polite assent.

"You fellers sleep warm?" Maguire's smirk was evident; it wasn't, in Spunky's eyes, meant in a gloating or superior way. A man simply acted the way Cactus Jack did after a night such as he'd had. Jack had his feelings, and they had theirs. Cap Donovan dashed his coffee dregs to sizzle at the fringes of the fire, his mood clearly darkened by Maguire's special favors but over which the young deputy had little choice. Cap, still very much a man despite his advanced years, seemed to speak for the others, but the edge in his voice was evident—almost a growl. "Not as warm, maybe, as you. But wasn't many of us as well fixed for camp comforts."

In his enthusiasm, Cactus Jack again missed any hidden meanings; that or he chose to ignore them. "It's a great day to be up and going after Ike Bodene. When're we going to fix some vittles and get back on the trail?" His questioning face was open and innocent.

Ryerson decided it was his turn. "You mean, Jack, that Mrs. Maguire isn't going to show up in a few minutes with tall-cut steaks all around and fried spuds and eggs?"

51

Maguire's face registered bewilderment. "Well, ah, no, Cole. Was you expecting that?"

An edge was evident in Ryerson's tone, too. "Just that I keep telling these boys what a thorough woman Bertha is. After the surprising events of last evening, one of her famous breakfasts was not outside the realm of possibility."

Cactus Jack surveyed the faces around the fire. "Well, ah, I don't think she had time yesterday forenoon to think about this morning's breakfast, too."

"We all understand, Jack," Ryerson said, again with his condescending tone. "Just that we all wasn't sure when all the surprises would be over."

"Bertha had me hitch up the team before daylight. You fellas was still sleeping," Maguire remarked apologetically. "The Ladies Aid at the church is puttin' on a supper this evenin', and she's agreed to make baked beans and potato salad."

Though what Cactus Jack described was hardly breakfast fare, five mouths nonetheless began to salivate around the fire.

"She's left already?" Ryerson inquired. "Knowin' her, she'll find time to mop the floors, too, when she gets home."

Cactus Jack missed the sarcasm. "No, Cole, today's her day to take the rugs out and beat them. She's prob'ly halfway back to Fort Walker by now."

Ryerson stared at his deputy helplessly. Then, stirring himself, he looked in disbelief in the direction the Maguires had camped. "Sure does beat all," he said under his breath. And then loudly, "Gentlemen, as you were. It would appear that this gawdam candy cotillion is over. Finish your coffee, douse the fire, and saddle up. There'll be a ration of corn pone and jerky while we ride. We have malingered here much too long. As Mr. Maguire has said, we need to get back on Ike's trail."

Spunky stayed squatted for the moment with his coffee cup, allowing that Ryerson was right. But, he thought, the last evening and its fine grub had sure as hell had all the earmarks of one of the finest he'd ever spent in camp or on the trail; the thought of having to pick up the way they'd began was not a little disconcerting.

He looked over to catch Dr. Hans Seabring's eye on him. It was plain from the good professor's expression that he harbored similar sentiments.

Two hours later they faced a barren, uninspiring wasteland relieved only by abundant clumps of dusty gray sagebrush and blue-green piñon and juniper. The land they'd camped in the night before hadn't much to recommend it, but at least there was a pothole now and then and a gravelly hummock or two to break the monotony.

Not much met the eye apart from a few distant buttes, hazy blue and so far west they tended to merge softly with the sky. Nearer, to the south—the way they rode—a stretch of dinky mountain range tried to rare up misty purple against a shimmering horizon, but not making much of a show of it.

Across the flapjack-flat terrain as sterile and devoid of beauty as though it was some of God's leftovers, the crossties and wear-polished high iron on the raised roadbed of the Southern and Central Railroad cut through the sage-choked land straight as a Sioux arrow.

Ryerson's Renegades converged for a council of war at the point that their trail intersected the twin threads of rail, spiked to legions of creosoted ties on a bed of gray slag and lavalike cinders and clinkers.

"Well, which way do we go, Cole?" Cap Donovan queried with irritation. "The day's getting on, and from the looks of the scenery, I for one am of the notion to tangle with Bad-Face Ike's boys pronto or go into camp early in some shady spot and lull myself into sweet dreams of peace with a noggin or two of that Group Tightener we're carrying on the pack-horses."

"Eloquently put, Cap," Ryerson remarked dryly. "Very eloquent! But just hold your horses. I'm cogitatin'. You're my tactician. Say you was an evil jasper the likes of Ike Bodene and you hit the train along here, which he did. Which way'd you go?"

Cap pursed his lips in thought. "Depends. On which way is the nearest water, shade, and serenity. And a good defensive position against the law and the *posse comitatus* sure to be on his back trail, like us. Sure not off there to the west and like the country we just come through, hard and dry and brittle as an old cast-off boot sole. The other way. That there now, that'd be my baseline."

Cole's head swiveled, studying the rail both ways, his face dark with thought, his features tight as ideas churned in his head. "South there, I guess," he said, gesturing with a flourish. "Up on Timberlodge. Those mountains look like runts from here, but there's

54

beautiful country up there. Tall pines the breezes sing through and the clearest, coldest crystal spring water you ever tasted or dunked a dink into. Its rejuvenative powers work miracles on the bather."

Cap Donovan grunted. "Now who's getting eloquent, Cole. Unless you've forgotten in your daydreaming reverie, Mr. Ryerson," he said with irritation, "we are here to run our outlaw Ike to ground and not to luxuriate over the healing qualities of some ice water spa."

Ryerson's face twisted again, his glinting eyes fixed on Cap. There was nothing he liked less than not being appreciated. "Well, forgive me all my gawdam transgressions, Cap. I merely tried to respond intelligently to your question."

"Meester Ryerson!" Fernando's voice piped up, insistent. "What is? Something there. East." All faces swung along the rail line in the direction Fernando pointed, his gaze fixed on the distance. Spunky shaded his eyes to see better.

At the edge of the horizon where the two glinting ribbons of iron rail tapered to a point and lost their definition against the shimmering, midmorning sun, two black moving specks floated in suspension above the land as though on a thin film of water. Clearly a chimera, a mirage effect that defied imagination as well as physical laws. "What the hell!" Ryerson roared. "Sure as little green apples the D.T.'s ain't getting to me! Dr. Seabring! Front and center!" The scientist urged his horse out of the pack of riders closer to their leader. "What do you need, Cole?"

"Someone or something's out there, coming along the rails. And it ain't a train." Ryerson spoke as though explaining his speculations to all. Then he turned to Seabring. "How long, Hans, would it take you to set up your telescope?"

Dr. Seabring studied and calculated the distance with the air of an artillerist plotting his range. "Long before whoever or whatever that is becomes distinguishable to the naked eye."

"If you can quick crank that monster down horizontal, Doctor, then proceed. Gentlemen! Get down and loosen cinches. We'll soon know if this is one of Bodene's tricks and prepare our strategies. For now, relax, have a smoke if you care to. Need any help, Doctor?"

"Perhaps Mr. Maguire could help me off-load and set up."

"Done!" Ryerson proclaimed, mocking Seabring's pontifical lingo. "Cactus Jack, if you ain't still too stove-up from last evenin's excesses in camp, you heard the man! See to *'off-doing'* them half hitches on the packsaddle with Dr. Seabring's telescope."

Spunky observed it all in amusement. Ryerson's esteem for his peculiar scientist may have bordered on worship, but Boot Hill Cole never let anybody get away with being snooty. Or snotty.

In minutes, with Cactus Jack scurrying to help, Dr. Seabring had unfolded and leveled his tripod and tightened the locking nuts of the big brass tube into a horizontal attitude. He screwed in his eyepiece, squinted through it, and began his focusing.

The specks in the distance by now had loomed larger, taking the form of a man on horseback, leading a second horse, probably a pack animal.

"He's alone," Ryerson proclaimed. "No point in

taking defensive cover. He won't try anything with so many of us facing him. Dr. Seabring, do you have a fix on the gent?"

"Come have a look-see, Cole. He's a white man, and from the looks of him, a woodsman."

Ryerson scooted over to crouch, hands on bent knees, over the giant polished brass cylinder, squinting into the small tube eyepiece, being careful not to jar the delicate instrument. "Face don't ring a bell," Spunky heard him mutter. "I can see him clear as if I stood up next to him. I'd say with almost certainly that he ain't any of Bad-Face Ike's slime." Ryerson stepped back. "Any of you fellas who never had the experience of peekin' through one of these things ought to come up here and have a good look at that jasper comin' yonder."

Spunky was closest and he took the initiative to step over to imitate Seabring's and Ryerson's stance behind the telescope eyepiece. The approaching rider filled the large glass tunnel of Spunky's squinted vision. The man was bearded and burly, tanned and robust from some hard occupation or other. He wore a dented gray felt hat that had once been a lighter color and a red-and-black-checked wool trail coat that had long since seen better days. A stocky roan provided his transportation. He led a thick-legged, stubby pinto with all the conformation of a mustang and fitted with a crude, wood-tree packsaddle; well-worn canvas panniers dangled from either side of the saddle tree.

Spunky stepped aside to allow Cactus Jack a look; the deputy studied the approaching rider, still an undistinguishable gray-black mass in the distance.

"I'll be switched," Cactus Jack enthused. "You can see him clear as day through there!"

Ryerson beamed. "See why I asked ol' Doc Seabring along?"

Cactus Jack stepped aside, and Fernando went to the telescope and crouched to squint through the eyepiece, palms on bent knees. *"¡Madre mia!"* Spunky heard him exclaim hoarsely.

In a few minutes, the rider came within hailing distance. "Seen you fellers from two miles back down the line," the burly rider yelled as he approached. "Got good eyes. I could always see a gnat or a nit on a buffalo's tit from forty rods off. Other times my eyesight's so bad I cain't find my prong with both hands. Need some of them bifollicle glasses. There's queer doin's afoot in this country. Evil men ridin' the land. You fellers ought to be more careful. What's that there thing you got there? You a survey party for the railway?"

"Nawsir," Ryerson responded, keeping his reserve until he had the jasper sized up.

"Looked like a mountain howitzer when I was comin' down the line back there, but up close any danged fool could tell it ain't. Can a man get down and stretch his legs and ease his hosses? I swear it's been a right smart piece from up on Timberlodge, and I ain't been out of the saddle since first light."

Spunky noted that, as with men who spend a great deal of time alone in the wastelands, their visitor was both garrulous and a fast talker, stringing his words together like beads.

"Light and squat a spell, stranger," Ryerson called.

58

"And, naw, we ain't in the employ of the Southern and Central. That there's a telescope."

"Telescope, y'say? That's for them scientist guys. Is that what that feller in the straw skimmer is, a scientist? Looks like one. Every one of 'em I ever seen wore them funny kind of spectacles." The rider dropped heavily out of the saddle and walked up and down a bit to straighten out the kinks. He stamped his feet to wake them up.

"Laws amassy!" he exclaimed. "I'm gettin' too old for that kind of ridin'. Name's Nesler. Dave Nesler. And you, sir? And your friends?" He spoke in Ryerson's general direction as though taking him to be leader of the gang of strangers.

Ryerson still held his offerings of information in check. "And what, Mr. Nesler, brings you out for a long ride like that in such sultry weather?"

Nesler eyed Ryerson suspiciously but sensed from the looks of Ryerson's Renegades that this group, like him, was of peaceful intent as far as he was concerned. "Well, sir, I'll get right to it first whack with you, stranger," he said. "I do a little hard-rock mining up on Timberlodge, if it's anything to you," Nesler said. "Headed for Fort Walker on business."

"You acquainted in Fort Walker, Mr. Nesler?" Ryerson asked. "We're from there. Don't believe I ever saw you in town."

Nesler continued feisty. "Well, with good reason! I don't go there oftener than I have to." Nesler peeled off his bulky trail coat and hung it from his saddle horn. His torso was covered by a threadbare and faded red union suit top from which some of his longer and coarser chest and shoulder hair sprouted like hog bristles; he hadn't had his underwear off for a long spell. Gray galluses, also once another color, supported work-worn Levis bloused over tall, once black stovepipe boots with mule-ear flaps to help pull them on.

"Got to go now," he continued. "Trouble up on Timberlodge. Evil doin's afoot. Going to go have a talk with the law in Fort Walker."

Cole Ryerson drew himself up tall. "Well, Mr. Nesler, I'm pleased to be able to save you a day-and-a-half ride." He made a great show of peeling back the lapel of his tan duster to expose his shiny circled star nickel-silver marshal's badge pinned to his black broadcloth suit coat. "As for the law in Fort Walker, you're talkin' to it!"

"You Cole Ryerson?! Well, why in hell didn't you say so in the first place?"

"It's a man's right to hedge his bets and not tip his hand until he's had a fair notion if he ain't going up against a stacked deck."

"I suppose I can't quibble with that," Nesler said.

"Don't pay to get too thick till you got the measure of a man. Now, what can the law from Fort Walker do for you?"

Nesler looked around. "You fellers got any coffee?"

Ryerson looked at the others incredulously. He swung his gaze back at Nesler. "You ain't ridin' clear to Fort Walker just to have coffee with me, are ya?"

"Well, for Pete's sake, no!" Nesler protested. "Just that some'd set good along about now."

"We had ours hours ago and wasn't figuring on

fixin' more on the trail. How'd a swig or two of some good old hundred-proof nose paint suit you?"

"Sure would smooth gettin' to the business at hand, Mr. Ryerson."

"Mr. Maguire!" Cole called. "Will you get out one of our jugs to pass around while we have our powwow with Mr. Nesler here. I sense the hand of our quarry in all this." Maguire leaped to action.

Cole went over to squat in an area away from the roadbed and clear of the ever present sagebrush and brittle tumbleweed. Nesler joined him while the others hunkered down at random but within hearing.

"Was about seventeen of 'em," Nesler began as Maguire strode up with a thick, blue glass bottle full of amber liquid. "Raided me yesterday evenin'. The jasper that seemed to be the ringleader looked like he'd been hit in the face at fifty yards with Number Nine buckshot before somebody run over it with a hay rake. He was a sight. Half-blood, prob'ly, or Meskin. Same thing."

Ryerson grinned at all the faces around him and Seabring gasped, "Ike Bodene!"

"Himself!" Ryerson proclaimed. "I can almost smell the bastard from here." His voice lowered. "Now, Mr. Nesler, there's Mexicans and there's Mexicans. It's been my experience that evil blood ain't particular what color skin it runs under. Fernando yonder understands every word you said."

"Meant no disrespect," Nesler apologized. "Ain't a good time for me." Nesler bit his lip and Spunky Smith, across from him, saw tears around Nesler's eyelids. "They killed Sal! Gawdam 'em, they killed

Sal!" he moaned with a sob in his voice. "She and me'd been together thirteen years! Had no notion of harm, for God's sake. Dear, sweet soul only meant to scare 'em off my claim. And they shot 'er for it! That one hit in the face with the BBs was the one that done it!"

"Sal? Your woman?" Ryerson asked, his voice heavy with concern.

"Woman!? No, dammit, my dog! Better'n any woman I ever knew. Cross between a Tennessee redbone coonhound bitch and a wolf stud. I'll never find another like her, and what's more, they took what few nuggets and flake gold I had sacked."

"We'll get your gold back for you, Nesler," Ryerson reassured, realizing how close he was to coming to grips at last with Bad-Face Ike. "And I'm real sorry about your dog."

"Hell, Ryerson, I can spare the gold. More where that come from. But the Lord didn't make but one Sal. That's why I lit out to find you and tell you. Couldn't stand bein' there without Sal just now."

"I know how you feel. Point is that this here *posse comitatus* is organized to track down this Ike Bodene, the very jasper that laid your dog low. I don't hold with dog-killin' any more than I do with train robbery. They're one and the same in my book, only differing slightly in degree."

"I'm beholden to you for your sympathies, Marshal."

"Where's your place? You can trust us. Just knowin' puts us lots closer to cutting Bodene's trail. If we can pick up his spoor from your claim, we could be slidin' the groove in Ike's direction before nightfall. Otherwise, we'd be chasin' our tails out here in no-man's-land for three, four more days."

"You can't miss it. Up Roughneck Pass Road about ten miles off Timberlodge Trail. Know the land up in there?"

"Mr. Maguire and I've done our share of scouting out that way. Yes, I can find it. Sure fine country up there on Timberlodge, ain't it? Inspirin'."

"None finer. Take more'n that speck-faced rascal to budge me off my claim! Now, sir, the southwest corner rock cairn of my claim is right at the edge of Roughneck Pass Road. You'll spot it easy. Got about a quarter section claimed, and my shanty and my mine shaft are about dead center. You go from that rock cairn due northeast, and you'll walk right through my front door. I'd go along and guide you, but I got to go to town for groceries. But you make yourselves to home at my cabin."

"If luck's with us, you may meet us on the way back, bringin' in the Bad-Face Ike bunch."

"And if I do I'm like as not to shoot the son of a bitch on sight!"

"I'd take it as a personal favor if you don't make my work any more of a nuisance than it already is," Ryerson said.

"Then I hope *you* have to shoot the son of a bitch!"

5

Timberlodge proved to be all Nesler and Ryerson said it was when, by late afternoon, Ryerson's Renegades were well up its evergreened slopes; the sun, a demon on the desert floor, was more respectful among the tree-shaded Timberlodge hills.

Here and there amid the pine, fir, and spruce, many of them leggy before they branched out to pay homage to the sky, bushy, low-growing cedars made their presence known by their distinct pungent aroma, strongly reminiscent of rich-smelling campfires, good times, good talk, and good friends.

After bidding farewell to Dave Nesler and mounting up for the ride west along the Southern and Central right-of-way, Ryerson withdrew into his thoughts. Spunky figured the heat had a bearing on Cole's sour disposition; it became an effort for any of them to talk, other than what needed to be said. Riding itself was a chore; even breathing was something a man wished he didn't have to do.

While others once in a while made a stab at conversations that quickly dwindled and died, Cole Ryerson only grunted when spoken to. Intelligible words from him were merely one at a time, and then only statements of one syllable, uttered as though he was angry about something—though they all knew he was not. There'd been no cause.

Spunky calculated that it was about eight miles from the rail line to the foothill slopes along a traveled avenue through the sage and chaparral, more of a tramped-down lane of well-packed granitic gravel.

He grew aware that the land graded up to the Timberlodge when Old Stockholder responded to the strain, lowering her head and making more of an effort to lift and set her feet.

The very demands of travel, and the uncompromising heat had lured Ryerson's Renegades into an indifferent frame of mind. The careful Rogers's Rangers tactics of the day before were forgotten in the mere desire to eat the scorching miles to what had been promised as an elysium for the jaded, heat-dazed desert traveler. They bunched together haphazardly or rode singly, following—dejectedly and almost blindly—the man riding point, Cole Ryerson. It hadn't occurred to any of them that their incautious attitude made them splendid targets for the likes of the wily Ike Bodene.

To the eternal good fortune of the *posse comitatus*, Ike's gang didn't stage an attack that afternoon.

Around them, craggy desert foothills rose to a region of stunted and stubborn scrub oaks, rugged, flinty runts with small, scalloped waxy leaves, as the terrain climbed steeply toward tall pines country. The twisty lane or road sprawled more broadly here, and Spunky had been aware that several trails across the arid desert below, coming in from several compass points, had merged. This must be, he thought, the Timberlodge Trail that Nesler had spoken of.

The squatty range, he also surmised, must be called the Timberlodge Range or the Timberlodge Mountains by the surveyors, topographers, and cartographers. But so far he'd only heard the place referred to merely as Timberlodge.

The tall pines and fir announced themselves with fragrance and soft murmurs against the prevailing winds before they were seen. Spunky also realized that for some time he had been aware of a more balmy quality in the air around him. The temperature hadn't moderated much from the noontime frying pan intensity of the desert; still the atmosphere among the tall evergreens had a clarity all its own and was more bracing.

Old Stockholder began to perk up too, her head erect, her step lighter, despite the fact that the steepness of the grade she covered with her human cargo hadn't decreased.

With the change in the land and the air around him, Ryerson's mood improved perceptibly and he unhinged his jaw. When he spoke to the other riders clustered around him, it was as though his five or six hours in the saddle almost incommunicado hadn't happened.

"Nesler's a lucky man," he declared loud enough for all to hear as he continued to lead them up Timberlodge Trail.

"That's sure enough right," Cactus Jack agreed naively, riding near the marshal. "It's a wonder Bad-Face Ike didn't just up and shoot him down like a dog."

"Like Sal," Spunky said.

"But it ain't a wonder," Ryerson interrupted. In his role as commander, he had more up his sleeve. Much more; an object lesson to his troop. They were seasoned fighting men, each in his own right; just now, though, Ryerson reasoned, they needed a leavening experience. And, to save his own hide—as well as theirs—he intended to deliver it, devil take the hindmost. "No wonder at all. Do you think after hoisting ten thousand dollars off the Southern and Central a week or so back that Bad-Face Ike really cared about old Nesler's few measly nuggets and maybe a little poke of gold flakes?"

"Well, Ike took it, didn't he?" Spunky put in.

"Oh, yeah," Ryerson responded. He glowed inwardly; like a dose of Epsom salts, his plan was at work. "He wasted a perfectly good .44 round on dear old Sal. Ike had no call to kill the dog and then turn Nesler loose without killing him, too. Not Ike's style. He was the man they wrote the book on bloodthirsty about. He kills with that fine word *impunity*. And those are the facts, gentlemen, upon which we must base our actions."

"So?" inquired Dr. Seabring.

Ryerson hit his stride. "And you call yourself a scientist, perfesser. I'm amazed," he said in an almost taunting tone. He put the second phase of his plan into action, and the men played directily into his hand. "A scholar of your renown in the area of deductive reasoning."

"What the hell has all this got to do with the price of beans in Boston, Cole?" Cap Donovan demanded. Ryerson's head pivoted, his eyes showering veritable sparks at Cap.

"And Captain Jeremiah Donovan, late of the great Texas Rangers. I'm surprised at you as well. Spunky and Cactus Jack and Fernando here are tough fighters, cool heads under fire. That's why they're along. But I had expected more of a man with a scientific doctor's degree and a Texas Ranger captain turned first-class lawman."

Seabring only looked bewildered while Donovan flashed a scowl at Ryerson that might've set tinder ablaze. "Well, you don't have to get so abusive about it, Cole! You're telling me that there's more here than meets the eye," Donovan said, matter-of-factly.

"Aha!" Dr. Seabring exclaimed.

"Old Hans has taken a grip on it!" Ryerson enthused. "I have been waiting since noon for it to dawn on you, Cap, but it hasn't. So I must be brutally blunt to keep you on your toes, Captain Donovan."

"I don't get it," Cactus Jack said.

"I hadn't expected it to hit you like a bolt out of the blue, Mr. Maguire. But I had anticipated more from these two esteemed gentlemen. This entire affair of late—killing Nesler's dog and leaving old Dave riled up enough to march right out and find me and get me out here fast—was cooked up as another part of this heinous plot by that crafty chili eater, Ike Bodene! This, gentlemen—somewhere up in here, amidst all this primeval beauty—is a territory where a gringo usually will drop his guard and tend to relax his vigilance. This is where Ike chooses to make his stand. This is where the cheese gets binding."

"Yeah," Spunky enthused, catching the drift of Ryerson's thoughts. "If he'd killed Nesler, we'd never have known it, would never have thought to come up here. We'd be days, maybe weeks, hunting Bad-Face Ike's trail. He's impatient. He needed a clear signal to send us."

Ryerson's eyes squinted in merriment that at last his Renegades had waked up. "Good for you, Sylvester. As I read the sign, Ike's as anxious as we are to get on with the carnage."

"A trap!" Donovan exclaimed. "Nesler was the live bait!"

"Not a trap, Cap," Ryerson said, still grinning as his plan meshed. "Claptrap!" Cole dug for his cigarette makin's. "A trap you blunder into. Bodene just sent us a deliberate clue as to his whereabouts so we can get this shivaree from a trot to a lope. He won't be hard to find now."

"Where's Nesler's claim from here?" Seabring asked.

"Roughneck Pass Road heads northeast along here soon," Ryerson responded. "Nesler said ten miles up or thereabout to the corner cairn of his claim. We'll make it before dark. From this point we ride defensively. Ike could set a real trap between here and there to pop us out of our saddles. And don't think for a minute he's not getting regular reports on our movements. As early as last evening, his sneak-scouts were prob'ly out there in the dark watching and listening in on our every movement." Spunky caught a sly twinkle in Cole's eye.

Cactus Jack reacted with shock. His words were stammered. "Do you really think so, Cole? I mean . . . even after we, ah, went to bed?"

Suddenly, Ryerson relished having his deputy in a box; a proper object lesson in discipline. "Naturally. I think Ike's bunch got eyewitness, step-by-step reports."

"Don't ever tell Bertha," Cactus Jack said hoarsely.

"The woods are thick all the way up," Spunky put in, seeing that the pressure on Cactus Jack needed to be relieved. "Perfect places for an ambush," Spunky added.

"Jack," Ryerson went on, ignoring Spunky. It was time for their comeuppance. "There's a stern code among gentlemen. What needs tellin' to wives or ladyfriends is left to the gent in question unless it's a matter of life and death or the man isn't in any condition to speak for himself. As for ambush, as Spunky has just so aptly reminded us, I have spent the afternoon at great risk of personal life and limb observing how the members of this here *posse comitatus* allowed the debilitations of a second day of insufferable heat and fatigue render them altogether indifferent to the dangers of just such a sneak attack and incapable of proper response. Gentlemen, you rode in here like a pack of rabble! We have discussed the need for observing Major Rogers's rules for the regulation of his Rangers. Yesterday you applied those principles with admirable skill. Let those words to the wise be sufficient. Henceforth, conduct yourselves as stouthearted men in the territory of a wily, vicious predator who will give no quarter, and no more will be said of it."

The riders looked at each other, bunched together like a gang of cow waddies discussing movement of a herd. Self-consciously, they reined their horses around to separate into a well-spaced platoon ready to ride on to the junction with Roughneck Pass Road—as well as to meet any emergency as Ryerson had charged, like stouthearted men. They stood to their positions silently and stoically, awaiting their leader's orders.

"Now," Ryerson commanded, his voice vibrant with renewed authority. "No sense in lollygaggin'! The sooner we confront the bastard, the sooner we get headed for home. Let's move out!"

"Hold your horses, Cole," Cap Donovan piped up. "I confess to military laxity on the ride up here brought on by the hardships of the march. But, nothing happened. Now, you retained me as tactician. So, let me advise here and now that if they strike as we travel, we'd better figure—as a fighting unit—to hit the dirt, hunt a hole or a rock or a tree, and give 'em as good as we get."

"Admirably put, Captain Donovan! Right out of Rogers's Regulations for Rangers, or at least close enough. It was Number Seven. The gist of it was, 'If you are obligated to receive the enemy's fire, fall, or squat down till it is over, then rise and discharge at them.' Again remember, gents, that Rogers was talking of muzzle-loading musketry. We can continue to lay low and fire from protected positions with our repeating rifles. He writes of our flankers driving in theirs, and further, that if 'disposition may be made for attacking, in the center, observing to keep at due distance from each other, and advance from tree to tree, with one half of the party before the other ten or twelve yards.' Gentlemen, in such an event, make every shot count. We've got to thin their ranks fast."

"We have six, Cole," Dr. Seabring put in. "Nesler counted for Bodene seventeen. Your Colonel Rogers postulates equal forces. By my computations, each of us needs to account for about three of the enemy."

Ryerson cranked his head slowly, studying each of them soberly. "So don't let anything happen to you. Get hurt or killed and you just double the work for those that's left standing. But may I remind you, Herr Perfesser, that one stouthearted man is superior to six or more yellow-bellied backstabbers such as Bodene has surrounded himself with. This explains why you were picked for this command."

"Brilliantly put," Dr. Seabring said, his tone facetious.

"Along those lines, I'll say this," Donovan added. "If we get pinned down, Bodene knows he has a superior force. We're convinced he's scouted our posse. He'll expect us to hole up and defend ourselves so they can decimate us piecemeal."

"I know you too well, Cap. Do I sense that there's more on your mind than just that now?" Ryerson asked.

"So you've read my mind, Marshal Ryerson. Do you mind telling me what it is?"

"We're of a like mind, Captain. A well-used but well-respected tactical phrase, 'The best defense is a good offense.'"

Spunky spoke up. "We ain't so bad after all. They got rocks and trees to hide behind. But we got rocks and trees on our side, too."

"But that's not enough," Ryerson said. "Cap's got the right idea. Give it to 'em, Cap. We're about to out-Rogers even Rogers!"

"If attacked, we should spend a few minutes defensively," Donovan began. "Holed up and secure. Test them. But make every shot count. See how well they shoot and where they shoot from. Determine the strength and emplacement of the enemy."

"Now we start to think like stouthearted fightin' men," Ryerson chimed in. "Never knew an outlaw or a *comanchero* yet that could shoot for dry owl shit. We got our ace in the hole right there. When it comes to fightin', we still got the edge. Stouthearted men! Ain't a one of that Ike Bodene bunch that ain't a pipsqueak. A damned pipsqueak. Take Ike himself. For all his depravity, a hot squaw and a cold camp'd kill that diabolical son of a bitch!"

"Pick out the three enemy positions closest to your zone of fire," Seabring advised with almost abstract, scientific statistics, seeming to ignore Ryerson's assessment of the enemy's lack of any redeeming values. "Take out those three, and then see to aiding your closest comrade. We will have at once the edge!"

Cap Donovan sounded excited, suddenly lusting for the kill. "You gonna give the command, Cole? When it's time to attack, I mean."

"Yeah," Ryerson said, his enthusiasm evident as well. "The rebel yell's the best. If you've never heard it, you'll know it in your gut when you do. Us Secesh horse soldiers used it to good advantage ridin' up

Graveyard Hill with Jo Shelby's horse cavalry charge at Newtonia, Missourah. Just pick up the yell and make the sound like I do. It's simple but positively effective. Ike's bunch probably never heard it, and I'll bet a new Stetson it'll scare the bejesus out of 'em! At least take 'em off guard. Two out of three of them chili eaters'll crap little adobe bricks."

"Then," Donovan pronounced, "up and out of your cover screaming like banshees and charge 'em, all horns and rattles."

Ryerson turned to Fernando. "You ain't got your two cents' worth in, amigo. Whatta you think about all this?"

Fernando fixed his unblinking dark Mexican eyes on Ryerson. "I wish I have the horn, how you say? The trumpet. I would play 'The Degüello' before we attack."

"The . . . huh?" Maguire asked.

"I wish he had a horn, too, if he could play it," Ryerson started.

"I could play it," Fernando assured, almost interrupting Ryerson.

"'The Degüello,' gentlemen," Ryerson went on, soberly. "I hope none of you ever has to hear it from an enemy pitted against you. Under such circumstances it must be a dreadful sound. The Mexican cutthroat song. Santy Ana had his band play it before the final charge of the Alamo. It pledges that no quarter shall be given. No survivors. The fight to the death. I heard it once. Mexican band in Waxahachie. Almost better'n the rebel yell for makin' the enemy's blood run cold. No words, just music. Bone-chillin'."

"I got it," Spunky chimed in. He'd listened to the

discussion with rapt attention. "Fernando ain't got a horn and we ain't musicians, but I got an idea. There's no point in hidin' any more. Bodene is waiting. And watching. And listening. Knows we're on his trail. Waiting for his advantage to attack. When we camp at Nesler's tonight, Fernando could teach us all the 'la-dee-dah' notes. That, or we can whistle it. Then, when we're ridin' Ike's trail, we can send him the message of the cutthroat serenade while we're on the move."

"Ike knows about it or for sure some of his own accursed throat-slitters do," Ryerson said enthusiastically. "He'll get the message. There's no notion what effect it will have."

Donovan was caught up with Spunky's inspiration. "Can you whistle, Fernando? I can't whistle worth a hoot. I only hum and carry a tune."

"And you can hoot, right, Cap?" Spunky quipped, remembering their previous night together on guard.

Fernando was one jump behind. "Sure!" he agreed. "Sure, I can whistle." Happily, he pursed his lips and began doing justice to the haunting notes, characteristically Spanish in their slow, measured dirgelike cadence, and trilling, sliding minor-key phrases. Spunky felt shivers along his spine, glad such music wouldn't be used against him. Soon Maguire chimed in, feeling his way along, following Fernando's lead with the music. Out ahead, Cole Ryerson boldly puckered up with a loud, commanding, and professional-sounding warbled whistle. Spunky wondered where Ryerson had learned such beautiful whistling; in all his years of knowing Boot Hill Cole, it was the first time Spunky had heard him whistle. He was magnificent at it.

Cole Ryerson, he mused, was a man of many hidden talents.

"Now!" that selfsame Ryerson commanded. "Trooop! Move out at a walk. Mah-arrrrch!"

Loudly whistling, humming, or trying their darnedest to "la-dee-dah" their way through the notes of "The Degüello," Ryerson's Renegades militarily spaced themselves in a column of twos but across the road from one another in strict adherence to Rogers's Regulations for Rangers. They rode as resolutely as seasoned cavalrymen, making the trees and rocks resound with their mournful, spirit-jarring "no quarter" message to Bad-Face Ike—emboldened and fused as they were by their common bond and this new display of their *esprit de corps*.

6

It seemed no time to Spunky before Ryerson threw back his head and commanded with booming cavalry-officer authority, "Col-yum lay-eft, mah-arrch!" The marshal reined Jo Shelby in that direction and waved his right arm to guide them. A leisurely twilight settled softly over the Timberlodge, the tall fragrant spruce and fir darkening with shadow; Spunky mused that it was a pleasant, yet dangerous, time to be riding.

"Welcome, gentlemen," Ryerson called in the same rich, stentorian voice, "to Roughneck Pass Road!"

Wheeling their column at a sensible walk behind Ryerson, his "Renegades" put new vigor into their whistled, hummed, sung and tone-deaf chanted version of "The Degüello." The die was cast for Ryerson's Renegades; from here on out, it was root, hog or die!

Their night fire twinkled through the dense dark of Dave Nesler's ample but sparsely furnished shanty, all but buried under the crowding trunks of great spreading and sky-seeking fir and pine of the Timberlodge slopes.

Virtually transfixed as he always was by night fires, Spunky watched the flames' tapered dancing fingers and allowed to himself that Dave Nesler was aptly named until calamity rode in with Bad-Face Ike; Nesler was nestled down in more peace and serenity in this place than any one man deserved.

"Best we don't build a fire out in the open and make sitting ducks of ourselves," Cap Donovan had offered as they dismounted and made ready for their second night on Bad-Face Ike's trail.

Cole Ryerson flipped a stirrup over his saddletree and began loosening Jo Shelby's cinches. "I don't see any sign of Mrs. Cactus Jack trundling along behind us tonight with another splendid feed," he remarked peevishly. "So it's salt pork and corn pone all around. Hans, you're good at stirring up laboratory chemicals and such and portioning things out with mathematical precision, so you can be Cookie tonight. I'll figure somebody else to hustle the grub detail tomorrow. We'll pass the chore around. Maybe we'll cut us out a first-rate camp cook on this here *posse comitatus.*"

In pairs for security, with Spunky and Fernando taking the first turn, they unsaddled and rubbed down their horses with gunnysacks, corned and grained them out of the packhorse supplies, and saw to their personal gear and bedrolls.

The two of them stumbled in the dense darkness, feeling their way. "Black as a club flush," Spunky grumbled. Under his skillful hand with the coarse burlap, Old Stockholder's hide twitched contentedly.

Spunky's mare all but purred placidly, enjoying being out from under the saddle in the cool night air, and the loving rubdown by the man acknowledged as master.

"I do not know this club flush," Fernando said. "Dark like night, hey?"

"Poker," Spunky responded. "I suppose you never played."

"But I always want to learn," Fernando said through the dark that separated them. "Nobody never show me."

Spunky's spirits brightened; he never knew a poker player yet who wasn't looking for a patsy. "You got any money, Fernando? I'll teach you."

"Sure, sure, I got some. How much it cost to learn?"

Spunky nearly said that it cost about what Fernando had in his pocket. He stopped, saying instead, "Depends." He said it cautiously, not wanting to spook an easy mark. "I'll show you. When we get some time." He shouldered his bedroll and war bag and groped for his heavy saddle to lug it into the cabin.

"Be sure to bring in your saddle, Fernando. I was lazy about mine one night when I was a greenhorn, and it made a prime picnic for a passel of porcupines."

"Or slippery fingers of señor Bad-Face Ike," Fernando added.

Spunky shrugged sardonically into the dark; Fernando had totally missed the fancy footwork of his words.

Nights turned cool on Timberlodge, it seemed, any time of the year, doubling the reason for keeping the shack's door closed. Moving around inside, silhouetted by the hearthside glow, a man could make a fine target for a sniper lurking in the dark.

Fernando, dragging his saddle and plunder behind Spunky, nudged the door shut with his heel and plunked his rig down in a likely spot to unfurl his bedroll. Fernando rummaged in his war bag for his mess gear.

They let the fire dwindle after supper. Ryerson, his white shirtsleeves and now open collar outlined by dim firelight against his black vest, nursed an after-supper cup of his bug juice as he paced up and down in front of a nest of embers in Nesler's fireplace. His posse men stretched out on their unrolled soogans or propped themselves against the cabin walls, little more than shadows in the pale light. Ryerson still wore his black chimney-tall Stetson to tower over his crew like Gulliver addressing a handful of Lilliputians.

Ryerson cleared his throat. "Now before any of you thinks of toddling off to the Land of Nod, we got to assign nighthawk duties on the remuda. And I hope each of you has secured your bangtail well on the picket rope out there in the dark. It'd be just like that sneaky weasel to crawl in here unbeknownst to us and run off our horses in the dark and leave us afoot." Ryerson raised his voice. "Mr. Maguire!"

Though he could not see him through the dark, Spunky sensed Cactus Jack stiffening to attention as he sprawled on his spread bedroll. "Mr. Ryerson," he responded.

"As my *segundo* on this here *posse comitatus,* and since you own a pocket watch, I will ask you to take the first shift in walking the guard line. In one hour you may come in and wake Mr. Smith to relieve you."

Maguire's form took shape in the waning firelight as he rose and looked around to determine Spunky's whereabouts in the jumble of men on Dave Nesler's cabin floor. He spied him sprawled on his open bedroll and nodded in confirmation. His left hand came up to finger the stiff, small white circle of tab on the drawstring of his Bull Durham sack; he touched his nearby nickel-plated deputy's star pinned over his heart to assure it was there, and dug in his vest's right breast pocket for his silver-cased watch. Cupping it in his left palm, he read the face, bending to favor the nearly nonexistent firelight.

"It's half past nine," he said, mostly by way of report to Ryerson.

"Very well," Ryerson said. "We rotate the shift every hour on the half hour, following Mr. Maguire's timepiece, which he will pass to his relief. We will sleep six hours, gentlemen, giving each man five hours of restful repose and one hour on nighthawk. We'll be up at three-thirty to breakfast, rig the horses and be ready to ride the trackdown trail at first light."

Without another word, Maguire tiptoed to the door, opened it, peered out cautiously and disappeared into the night, easing the door shut behind him. Spunky wondered momentarily if he'd been right in holding his tongue when he saw Maguire make sure of his cigarette makings. Naw, he thought, smoothing his bedroll and making ready to slide in; Cactus Jack's a savvy *hombre*. He won't go lighting any matches out there in the dark.

Ryerson's voice again boomed out of the darkening

calm of the cabin. "There being no new business to come before this assembly, I declare a recess until three-thirty tomorrow morning. Pleasant dreams, gentlemen." Ryerson's last words were mumbled and labored as he bent to struggle out of his boots. He and Spunky and the others went about the job of snugging their soogans around them, pulling up the canvas top sheet and folding and tucking the sides securely against the cold and whatever varmints might come scooting across the packed dirt floor to sneak in and share a man's warmth. And maybe some of his blood.

After a brief time of deep and dark oblivion, Spunky emerged into the light of full day, blissfully alone aboard Old Stockholder riding the Timberlodge heights, a silent land under a balmy, benevolent sun. Its diffuse, yellow presence only intensified the blue-green boughs of a legion of monarch pines and firs stretching toward the sky and away from him in all directions as far as his eye could see in the rolling hills that verged on being called mountains. He sensed none of Old Stockholder's hoof falls, and no rhythm to her gait. Instead, his mount flowed like calm water over a pleasantly thick brown-needled carpet of forest floor. Spunky sensed peace and serenity fill his heart. He felt the sort of ease that he was sure must dominate the life of Dave Nesler. Over and around him, like a hushed hymn of everlasting love of a bygone day, a comforting wind combed the high tree tips, lulling him to warm and good thoughts of just being alive; world without end, a-men.

Abruptly, like a force of evil exploding from the hellish depths below with nightmarish fury, the ground under him leaped and shuddered in a cataclysmic rage. Above him, the sky was rent with deafening thunder; the giant trees crashed and whipped against the pummeling of a howling, elemental wind. Terrified, Spunky was hurled from Old Stockholder's back to crash against rock-hard ground, his wits and breath slammed out of him. As sense returned, his eyes flickered open to the stark realization that the fall had blinded him; the sun and the day were gone, and all around him was an abyss of incredible blackness. His hands groped out of an entanglement binding him to earth; in a spasm of panic, he cupped his palms over his sightless eyes.

"What the hell was that?!" A frenzied voice knifed into his hearing from out of the black void.

"Sounded like a howitzer." Spunky recognized Cap Donovan's voice as dark forms gradually took shape around him; maybe he wasn't blind after all. His vision improved.

"Warn't neither. More like a .30/30," Cole Ryerson piped up. Wan light from the ruby bed of coals in the hearth softly outlining Dave Nesler's cabin walls glinted on the barrel of a Colt Navy in Ryerson's big mitt pointing skyward at the ready as the big marshal eased to the cabin door to cautiously shove it open onto the black night. A crisp gust of fresh air swirled into the cabin to refill Spunky's tightened lungs and to refresh a staleness created by nearly a half dozen heavy sleepers snoring as deeply as they slept.

Ryerson waited a long moment, watching through the thin slit of open door into the dark beyond topped by a silent, star-speckled sky, ears perked for voice or movement, anything. Others, Spunky included, were up with weapons drawn and safely pointed skyward as well, thronged behind Ryerson, quietly trying to peer past him into the night, ready to back him if more gunfire erupted.

"Who's out there on nighthawk?" Ryerson whispered at those crowding behind him. "Spunky?"

"Right here," Spunky answered. "Cactus Jack never woke me. Must be he's still on guard."

Ryerson called cautiously into the cool night air. "Maguire?" In anticipation of another bullet, he stepped away from the open door to await a response. He stood stoic a long moment before shoving his face into the door's narrow breach. "Hey, Cactus Jack? You all right?" His call was met by silence from out of the night.

"Maguire probably heard something and he took a shot in the dark," Dr. Seabring assured, trying to sound positive, a scientist's characteristic response until he has empirical data to the contrary.

"He's prob'ly huntin' around out there to see what it was," Spunky encouraged, wanting to think the scientist was right but, remembering Maguire thumbing his Bull Durham tab, felt his heart sink within him.

"Like hell!" The impatience of grave concern rang strong in Ryerson's voice as he spoke over his shoulder. "I still say that sounded like a .30/30. Cactus Jack went out of here with only his .44 hogleg Colt. Any damned fool knows the difference when they go off. He was shot at!"

"Calm down, Cole," Cap Donovan said right behind Ryerson as he tried to see out into the dark night over Ryerson's shoulder. "Don't jump to conclusions."

"Well, then, we got to get out there and look. I don't favor the sound—or maybe the stillness—of all this." Ryerson spoke with more apprehension tingeing the timbre of his usually assured voice. "I got a bad feeling. My gut's talking again. Cap, you and Fernando come on out with me and help hunt for Cactus Jack. Hans, you and Spunky get ready to back our play from in here. Take a few shots at the planets if there's a ruckus, just to make sure you don't take a chance shooting a pardner. But that kind of show of force might spook the bastards. Kick up that fire and dig out one of our jugs. I got a bad hunch we may need both. Dammit!"

With Ryerson, Fernando, and Donovan slipping silently into the night, Spunky took charge. "Hans, I'll cover them from the door. You roust up the fire and see to finding some of Cole's hootch, like he said." It was the first time he had called Dr. Seabring by his first name and suddenly he wasn't altogether sure he hadn't overstepped his bounds; after all, the man was a doctor, a class Spunky always felt secondary to.

"Bully!" Seabring enthused to Spunky's great relief and gratitude. The doctor disappeared into the blackness of the cabin while Spunky returned his attention to the door opened barely a crack. Through it he shoved his nose and six-gun barrel. As yet he hadn't had time to think through his sweet dream of peace that had turned so suddenly and so violently into nightmarish proportions. The narrow door opening began to thrust a thin and wavering yellow bar of light into the night as the energetic little scientist stirred the fireplace embers to life and threw on new sticks and logs.

Spunky grew aware of movement and rustlings and cracklings of branches and dead pine needles and of soft calls in the dark. He heard a loud cry.

"Meester Ryerson! Over here!" and a long pause and more stirring around in the dark. Then,

"Great Christ!" Donovan's voice knifed into the night.

"Jack? Here, you, Cap! Take hold of his arm. That side, dammit! Fernando, lift his legs. Come on! Be quick!"

Spunky heard more thrashing around in the dark and hurrying footsteps approached the cabin. "Thank God we found the goddam place! Light from that goddam door sure helps. Lucky we even found this man!" Ryerson's voice boomed out of the oblivion of darkness. "Spunky! Open the damned door!" The three of them burst in, breathless, toting a very dead Cactus Jack Maguire. In the leaping firelight, Spunky saw with shock that something dreadful had happened to the side of Maguire's head.

7

They gently laid the dead man down on his rumpled bedroll close to Seabring's renovated fire. Ryerson looked into the lifeless face, unbelieving, as he straightened Cactus Jack's legs and crossed his hands on his chest.

"Cole, it don't make no difference now." Donovan's voice was as heavy as his heart; the first of Ryerson's Renegades had bitten the dust and it cut Donovan to the core. "Jack's dead."

Spunky was surprised that Cap's pronouncement of the obvious didn't bring an outburst from Ryerson. His reaction instead was uncharacteristically subdued in his shock and disbelief.

"Yeah, I know. It just seems like the decent thing to do." Ryerson's words were uttered with low, measured tone, his eyes rolling soulfully up at Cap towering above the slumped, beaten marshal. Ryerson hovered over the lifeless John Jacob Maguire as though tenderness and care at this point might exorcise the demon of death. Then softly, as though murmuring to himself, so softly, in fact, that the others scarcely heard, "My stouthearted men are outsmarted men." For a moment, his body shook with silent sobs. Abruptly, Ryerson squared his shoulders and, still kneeling beside Maguire's body, pulled himself erect. "Spunky Smith!"

"Yessir!" Spunky came out of a dark reverie that all this was still part of his recent nightmare. Yet he was realist enough to know it wasn't.

"There has been gunfire, and a spooky line of horses is picketed out there without a guard. You were assigned second watch. Do your duty!"

Spunky blanched. "Me, Cole? They've killed one man already!"

Spunky's protest was interrupted by the voice of Dr. Seabring. "Cole! Look here. On Maguire's shirt, this black thing!"

The dead man's shirt and vest were blood-spattered; a pencil-sized black mark about an inch and a half long lay on his shirt collar and onto the lapel of his vest.

"Burn mark, by God," Ryerson said, his bitter bout with grief put aside in favor of appropriate and decisive authority. "What do you make of that? Ain't powder burn."

"He was smoking, Cole," Spunky said gravely. "Bad-Face Ike's sniper took a bead on his cigarette tip. Looks like when he fell over, the cigarette lit on his shirt and burned it. I warned him against lighting matches in the dark our first night out when we were walking the guard line."

"I loved that man," Ryerson confessed, the catch back in his voice. "A prime deputy, but I guess we've all got weaknesses of the flesh. It was just that his need for a smoke got in the way of his good judgment."

Ryerson was silent a long moment, and Spunky delayed going out, fiddling with his gun belt and settling it more comfortably on his hip. He hefted his Winchester, thinking about having to go outside. If Bodene's sniper opened up again, he might see the muzzle flash and get a round off, or he might not live to see the muzzle flash at all. He knew he fidgeted nervously in his reluctance to leave the cabin. Ryerson saved him.

"Spunky! As you were! Men, we've all, most of us, slept with the dead in our time, on the battlefield or the outlaw trail. But out of respect for Mr. Maguire and our own hazardous circumstances, I suggest that we all sleep outside the rest of the night, wide apart, guns handy, ready to back the man on watch."

He dug in the dead man's vest for his pocket watch. "Spunky, just about now he'd've woke you for your turn. Now the rest of us will join you. You call me at eleven-thirty."

"Guess I'm relieved about that, Cole. Wasn't too anxious to wander around out there in the dark all by myself."

"It's still risky, so don't get lazy."

"At least I'll have company," Spunky said.

"Gentlemen, you have your orders." Ryerson paused, thoughtfully. "Wait a minute. Gather round. I didn't think, boys. We can't start out at first light after Ike Bodene!"

"And I'd like to know why not," Donovan said,

almost indignantly. "He's got some answering to do for shooting Maguire down with no more mercy than he showed Dave's dog, Sal. Money stealin's one thing. Murder's another."

"And right there's where the shoe starts to pinch, Cap."

"Meaning?"

"Meaning what do we do with Cactus Jack's body? That throws a couple more flies into the ointment."

"So, what do we do, Cole?" Spunky put in.

"That's what's giggin' me just now, son. I don't know. I flat don't know. Blame it on this damnable turn of events. If I can sleep after this, I need to sleep on it and tackle it in the morning fresh with a good cup of hot coffee. For the rest of the dark hours, we shall consider ourselves still under siege from Bad-Face Ike's backshooters. Let's not lose anybody else."

Ryerson hastily wadded up his soogans and tarp and, ramming the bulky, haphazard roll under his arm, strode boldly out the door of Nesler's cabin. The rest quickly followed his lead, leaving the firelight to flicker on the corpse of Cactus Jack Maguire.

As if to spite the tragic events of the night, dawn came fresh, bright, and promising. Spunky viewed it through the trees from the warm and snug vantage point of his bedroll. It had not been his best night's sleep ever. He was frazzled when he rolled up; his rest disturbed by his sweet-dream-turned-nightmare, the abrupt, tragic, and almost personal—he remembered good friends dropping next to him in war, lumps of instant death abandoned in the chaotic frenzy—bushwhacking of Cactus Jack, an exhausting, dragging hour on nighthawk, waking a grumpy and morose Ryerson for his turn at watch, and then wakeful off and on the rest of the night over the desperate turn of events.

Careful not to move radically and destroy his labored tucking in of the night before, and reluctant to depart his warm cocoon, Spunky pivoted his head, resting as it was on his saddle. Around him the camp was alive with movement.

A raucous voice intruded on his sleepy brain. "Well, well, Mr. Smith." It was Cole Ryerson. "At last you join the living! Everybody idled in their bedrolls this morning, but you're the last. Roust out, bucko, take your relief and get some of Dr. Seabring's miraculous coffee. It's time for a council of war!"

Spunky had little use for people who were bright and frisky first thing in the morning; Cole Clement Ryerson was one of those people, and Spunky hated him for it, especially since Ryerson woke up to Spunky's nudge like a disgruntled bear a little before midnight for his turn at nighthawk.

Coffee cup in one hand, Winchester in the other, Spunky circled up with other Renegades around Ryerson, seated on the giant trunk of a fallen tree, settling and rotting into its once nurturing land at the edge of Nesler's clearing. Behind and around them, forest trees were ranked on the sloping land nearly as thick as the palisade logs of a frontier fort. Behind Ryerson, a few steps away among the trees, a devoted Fernando and his Winchester disappeared and reappeared as he strolled a quarter circle guard line outside the clearing's perimeter.

"All right," Ryerson began. "Time for some drastic decision-making. I got Fernando backing us, but I'm not too worried about a dry-gulcher in daylight. The jackass that laid for Cactus Jack last night had to've been just about out in the open. Like I told you, outlaws ain't usually got much for shootin' eyes, so he must've been damned near on top of Maguire.

"But enough of that. The tragic events of last night presents us with a whole grab bag of new problems. Most pressing is the disposition of the body of the deceased."

"Was you thinking of taking him home, Cole?" Cap Donovan interrupted.

Ryerson fixed a blistering gaze on the aging Cap. "And where, Captain Donovan, is *your* head? What sort of a whiffy mess do you think you'd have when you got in, after most of two days across that fryin' pan of a desert we left yesterday? And I do not begin to speculate on the flies he'd attract and the wiggly, seething mess after they swarm over a dead body. Need I mention that ugly word, maggots? We've all been too many times in the camps of the dead under summer heat. I'll not allow that indignity to desecrate the memory of Cactus Jack Maguire!"

Cap Donovan hadn't expected such a sermon. "Well, I just wondered what you were thinking, Cole."

"Sour as the decision-making has to be, Captain Donovan, our only course is to bury him up here at Dave's. And that drops me smack-dab into another hell of a problem. More than a problem, it's giving me an acute case of the fantods."

"Which is?" Dr. Seabring asked.

Ryerson's gaze, his eye sparkling, fixed on his

scientist friend for a moment before coursing the circle of his posse men. "Bertha Maguire."

"I hadn't thought of that," Spunky said.

"She's gonna pitch a hissy when she finds out her man's dead," Ryerson went on. "But that'll be nothing to the fireworks if we wait till we get back to let her know. Which may be days. Or weeks. Bodene is doing his best to present us with a pesky job of work, gentlemen."

It was Dr. Seabring's turn to speak up. "Do I take it, Marshal, that you've formulated a plan, yes?"

"Nothing I'm very pleased with, Hans. All I know for certain is that before we can get on with running that murdering son of a bitch to earth, we're going to have to give Cactus Jack the most proper send-off we can up here. All these trees around us and no way to build him a decent box. Like that old shipwrecked mariner and all that ocean and nothin' fit to drink. So ol' Cactus Jack'll have to be content with his bedroll tarp for a shroud. Nesler's got picks and shovels roundabout, so we'll have no trouble puttin' down a decent hole."

Ryerson was silent a long moment. "I'll get Fernando going on it pronto. Doc, you and Cap and I can spell him."

Spunky broke in with, "You forgot about me, Cole. What about me?"

Ryerson fixed his gaze on Spunky for several moments without a word; a wave of sinking apprehension emptied Spunky.

"That's the part I'm havin' a hell of a time comin' to grips with, Spunky. Somebody's got to go all the way back to town and tell Mrs. Maguire."

"But . . ." Spunky protested.

"No buts or ifs or ands. You're the one I decided on."

"Why me?"

"Because it's got to be somebody, and it couldn't be me. I really can't spare you, but I'll be less troubled if I know the word is getting to Bertha, and I've decided in my mind that you're my man to do it. And I want you back here at a high lope. But since this is above and beyond the call of the duty of this *posse comitatus,* I'm giving you a bonus and permission to take time to go on a larrup while you're in town."

Spunky looked around him; he wasn't sure if the look Cap Donovan gave him was envy, but he took it for that and began to feel easier about Ryerson's assignment. The longer the idea dwelled in him, the better he felt about it. Then he started to sink all over again. The whole notion of facing her really didn't have that much appeal.

"Roll up your soogans and your war bag and get riding, Spunky. Bad-Face Ike is roundabout, so probably till you get back, this'll be base of operations. Do like I told you and then hit the return trail."

"What'll I say to her, Cole? I never had to tell a lady something like this before."

"You'll find the words, Sylvester. You got about two days to muddle on it. It'll take about that long to get to town."

Spunky decided to try one more time to discourage Ryerson. "But, Cole, Doc Seabring's educated. He'd know the right words to . . ."

"You're the man for the job, Spunky."

"Cap Donovan's a man of the world. Been in a lot more scrapes like this than I ever . . ."

"Shouldn't you be looking into saddling up Old Stockholder, Spunky?"

"Cap's a lot older, and Doc's a college man. Cole, I can dig a right smart better grave for Maguire than either of . . ."

"Dally your tongue, son, and rig for ridin'. Look at it this way, you're gettin' a furlough, all expenses paid. You merely got to stop by a few minutes and explain things to the Widder Maguire. The rest of whatever time you're there you can do a proper job of raisin' a little hell and have 'em put it on my bill. Just be bright-eyed and clearheaded next mornin' to get ridin' the desert and back here *muy pronto.*"

"But . . ."

"No ifs, ands, or buts, remember, Spunky? You got your orders."

Forty minutes later Spunky Smith found himself on Old Stockholder riding down Roughneck Pass Road headed toward the downside of Timberlodge Trail and the desert below. The ride had none of the glories of his blissful dream of peace the night before.

His jaw was set, his face muscles tense over his distasteful assignment, eyes angrily a-squint. "First time," he grumbled and muttered to himself, aware of the grand trees around him but now not seeing their stately, primeval beauty. "First time I ever knew Cole Ryerson to talk out both sides of his mouth. First he says she's gonna pitch a hissy, and prob'ly he knows them fireworks he spoke of is gonna be closer to the truth.

"Then he's got the sand to talk me into all this, tellin' me just to stop by her house and spend a few minutes explaining to her like I was the parson comin' to call about an ice-cream social at the church.

"Personally, I think it's gonna be more like a Yankee artillery barrage."

8

After any time in the open, the stifling confinement of streets and buildings of a town left Spunky feeling boxed-in, suffocating him to the edge of panic. The size of the place didn't make much difference; small town, big town—it was always the same. The blood pounded in his temples as he rode in, his hands all sweaty on the reins. At first the air was hard to breathe, as though too many people had already used it; he was afraid that any minute he'd start gasping or wheezing. After a while he adjusted to being there and the knotting-up relaxed. But the longer he'd been out—and the older he got—the stronger he felt it and the longer it lingered.

Spunky figured he felt small and inadequate in a town; this was where the sharpers and the scheming merchants operated, and Spunky allowed that mostly he was an easy mark for a glib tongue. And it scared him. Out in the country now, that was his place. A man could breathe deeply and swing his arms wide.

The code out there was simple; his gun was his justice and his meat-getter, and the land provided most of the rest of his groceries.

And he was elated to discover that just about the finest place for all those things he'd ever seen in the world was out there in Cole Ryerson's Fort Walker country—up on Timberlodge, inspiring surroundings. Already he missed it. Maybe, he thought, he'd at last found a home, a place to settle.

Dusk deepening over Fort Walker dulled its rough edges and softened its rutty main street, making it a bit more tolerable when he rode in on Cole Ryerson's errand. Spunky was relieved, too, that it was late, and paying a call at this hour on the widow who didn't yet know she was one would be improper.

He sought out the boardinghouse where he'd stayed when he came to town in response to Cole Ryerson's summons. Six bits in advance paid for an ample, private room and supper and breakfast downstairs, which was about all he'd need.

He'd only been out five days, so his craving for a jubilee over drinks and a few hands of poker wasn't strong. There were those in town who could have seen him earlier with Ryerson and Maguire and might come out with questions he wasn't prepared to answer. The burden of Cactus Jack's death and Spunky's unresolved quandary over how to approach the widow dulled his desire to celebrate being back in Fort Walker's bright lights and hoopla—of which there really wasn't much, Spunky allowed.

Instead, he financed a hot bath and a shave in the boardinghouse basement and paid the landlady's grandson a nickel to bring him a ten-cent quart pail of cool beer from McCurdy's Saloon down the street. He spent another nickel to rent a grimy deck of cards from the proprietress for an evening of solitaire, clean and cross-legged in his underwear on his threadbare quilt coverlet, basking in the soothing glow of a coal-oil lamp on the stand beside his bed.

The beer caused him twice during the night to drag out the thick and squat porcelain night vessel from under the bed and crouch over it like a small boy who hadn't yet learned to stand like a man. Then he tossed and turned trying to get back to sleep, his mind a seething cauldron of quandary about the Widow Maguire. In the morning, he fished out his clean Levis and brand-new shirt from his war bag and tried to figure how in the hell he was going to approach the woman.

The Maguire place was easy to find, and he wished it weren't. Even if he hadn't known where it was, he knew that all he'd have to do was look for the tidiest place in town and that would be it. Bertha had had Cactus Jack build a narrow board sidewalk in front of their little home on a side street, maybe the only residential sidewalk in town. The sidewalk was backed by a carefully spaced, pointed, and white-washed picket fence. A similar board sidewalk led from the gate to the front door. Through the religiously polished windowpanes that Spunky had heard so much about, he could see gossamer white curtains carefully tied back. Cactus Jack's house had a tin roof, its clapboard siding a fetching light blue, recently repainted. The roof's facia boards and the window and door frames as well as other trim wood, were accented in white paint.

The overall look of the place reminded him of Ryerson's remark that Bertha Maguire was "a very thorough woman."

Behind the house, Spunky could see a well-kept stable-barn; out of his sight but not his hearing came the familiar clucks and brooding croaks of Bertha Maguire's chicken yard, which he imagined was also fastidiously maintained.

For a long moment, Spunky stood before the picket gate, ready to lift the latch and go knock on the front door. He hadn't been seen and maybe, he thought in a spurt of panic and loss of resolve, he could go away and come back later. He'd ought to go somewhere and have a drink and think a little more about what to say. No sooner had he made the decision than Bertha Maguire herself came around the side of the house, a galvanized pail of steaming water in one hand and a wad of soft, absorbent cloths in the other. It was likely her day to wash the outside of her windows.

Spunky, caught unawares, turned tongue-tied.

But not Bertha. "Mister, if you're selling something, we don't want any."

"No, ah, Mrs. Maguire . . . I, ah . . ." Spunky stammered.

"Why, it's Mr. Smith, isn't it? Marshal Ryerson's friend?"

"Well, ah, yes'm . . ."

"I thought you were riding with Mr. Ryerson and Mr. Maguire and the others." She set her pail and rags down and came closer.

"I'm, sort of, ma'am . . . here now."

"Have you all come back? Where's John?"

"No, ah, no, I'm alone."

"Forgive my bad manners, Mr. Smith. Would you like to come in?"

"I reckon that'd be nice, Mrs. Maguire."

Bertha opened the gate for him and led the way up the walk to a low stoop at the front door. "You'll have to forgive me and the appearance of my house. I wasn't expecting callers."

The inside of the Maguire house was small, but clean, cool, and inviting. The night of her supper for the posse, he'd not taken much notice of the home or its furnishings. Spunky realized that he had sort of assumed that because of the way she kept house, her furniture would look like it just came from the store and never been sat on. Instead, there was a beckoning warmth and casualness in the furniture and its placement, the pictures on the walls and the curtains and other touches; a right homey little place, Spunky allowed, and said so.

"Nice place you've got here, ma'am." Spunky stood inside the door bashfully holding his battered Stetson over his crotch.

"John's as much responsible as I am, Mr. Smith. Would you like to sit down."

Spunky took a seat on the nearby sofa, nervously crossed his legs and perched his hat on his knee. Bertha sat in an overstuffed chair across from him.

"Now, Mr. Smith, what brought you to my door? How is Marshal Ryerson's search proceeding? And surely you bring me some word from Mr. Maguire."

"Well, Mrs. Maguire, I, ah . . ."

Bertha was silent a long moment. "Something's

happened. He's been hurt, hasn't he? I'm a strong woman, Mr. Smith. You needn't beat around the bush."

"It's a . . ." Spunky hesitated again. Just saying she was strong didn't make it so. Still he braved it out. "Not good."

"Mr. Maguire's been killed?"

"That's what you might say is the long and the short of it." With the saying of it, Ryerson's words rang in Spunky's head, "Bertha will pitch a hissy."

Instead, her eyes closed and she turned prayerful. "Lord, he was mine; now he is thine." When she opened them, her expression was grim, her eyes thoughtful. "The mister loved his work, and he was very devoted to Marshal Ryerson. There was hardly a morning, Mr. Smith, that Mr. Maguire got up from my breakfast table and left this house that I didn't get down on my knees and pray the Lord to return him safe again at day's end. A lawman's wife lives with such fears. She is careful not to reveal them to her man lest it cloud the performance of his responsibilities. A man troubled at home is half a man at his work, double danger for a lawman."

"Yes'm," Spunky acknowledged with great relief; Bertha was taking it a great deal better than he had expected.

"I'll be very blunt with you, Mr. Smith, since you seem to have been nominated as the bearer of the bad tidings. There was love between Mr. Maguire and myself, a deep, strong, and abiding love. In many diverse and wondrous ways we provided for one another's needs . . ."

Spunky saw a faraway look in Bertha Maguire's

eyes; her tracking Ryerson's posse clear down into the desert with a splendid chicken dinner mostly for the sake of sharing a bedroll with her husband and lover in the sand and under the stars all at once took on greater significance.

"Forgive me and understand if I do not wail and keen like an Indian squaw or swoon dead away like one of my weaker white sisters. My faith and my upbringing gird me, as do twelve years with a man devoted to me as well as to upholding the law and with the gun, if necessary. He did his duty as God gave him to see his duty in the brutal world outside this home. My duty was to make his inner world—this home—as comfortable, serene and gratifying as time, energy, love, and devotion allowed."

Bertha Maguire's eyes probed deeply into those of Spunky Smith. "In my eyes, Mr. Smith, grief is a debilitating, wasteful emotion. I was and am eternally grateful that the Lord provided me with twelve good and gratifying years with John Maguire. Are you a devout man, Mr. Smith?"

"Well, I, ah, Mrs. Maguire . . ." Spunky suddenly found his voice. "I like to think of myself as caring and compassionate and upholding of Christian principles, ma'am." The words flowed out of him. Somehow the woman's strength gave him power.

"Good, Mr. Smith. Your life on the range keeps you for the most part away from the House of God; you don't get to church often."

"Ah, no ma'am. But that don't diminish . . ."

"Then you will understand. I have thought this often as Mr. Maguire left my breakfast table day upon day to do his duty to bring justice to the frontier. In many respects, he was doing the Lord's work; most of the men he helped bring to justice had broken the Commandments. John might not have interpreted it in quite my terms, but the end result was the same."

"Yes'm." Spunky forgot Ryerson and Old Stockholder and the Timberlodge and almost everything as he hung onto the magic of her words and her voice.

"The Bible admonishes us to 'avenge not yourselves' and not to give place unto wrath. It advises that 'vengeance is mine' and that 'I will repay, saith the Lord.'"

Spunky was moved to an emphatic "amen"—and he meant it.

"I'm also a firm believer, Mr. Smith, that under certain circumstances, we may interpret the Scriptures as allowing us margin to assist in supporting the power of the Word of God—as my dear, departed husband did in his day-to-day work."

"Oh, yes'm." Spunky now leaned forward on the sofa, holding his hat, listening eagerly to Bertha's every word.

"Bad-Face Ike Bodene has deprived me of my lover and provider. Now I mean to do everything in my power to see that he is brought to God's great judgment seat."

"Oh, Mrs. Maguire. You surely can leave that to Mr. Ryerson and the others. This Ike Bodene will be brought up on charges—larceny and murder—you can rest assured of that."

"With my help!"

"Oh, yes, ma'am. I'll tell Cole Ryerson myself of your determination to see justice done."

"That, of course, Mr. Smith, is quite totally and

altogether beside the point. I'll require at least two days to prepare. I will appreciate your waiting in town to accompany me."

Spunky bounced back to reality with a jolt; he wasn't prepared for what he heard. "But, Miz Maguire! You can't go."

"Mr. Smith, you've not listened. I *will* accompany you back to Mr. Ryerson. I'll be there to help bring Ike Bodene and his scoundrels to justice. To take John's place, as it were. Also Mr. Maguire spoke so often of the quality of rations on the trail. I have an ample larder and pantry and my preparations will assure that you men are properly sustained in your quest. That said, Mr. Smith, I'll hear no more protest. In two days, at first light, you may call for me here at my front gate."

Spunky was aghast. "But, Miz Maguire, you've no place out there. This is a man's business, and not just any man either. Stouthearted men. Like Cole Ryerson's posse. Besides, Cole'll likely skin me alive if I'm not back there day after tomorrow. There's no tellin' what he'll do to me after that if you come riding in with me!"

"First light, day after tomorrow, Mr. Smith."

Spunky's astonishment turned to obstinacy. "I'm sorry. I'll not risk it, Mrs. Maguire."

"Very well then. Leave now. Go back, Mr. Smith. In two days, I ride to bring the Lord's vengeance to the killer of my lover and provider, John Maguire. If anything happens to me, my blood will be on your hands and those of Marshal Cole Ryerson!"

Spunky tried another tack. "Aw, Mrs. Maguire! Hadn't you ought to reconsider?"

"My greatest contribution can only be with you and Marshal Ryerson's posse. If you scorn me, Mr. Smith, my need will be doubled to personally confront that Bodene man. With you or without you."

Spunky turned irritable. "Why don't you wait till I ride back and explain to Cole? If he says it's okay, I'll come back for you."

"And consider the wasted days that Bodene is abroad on the land, scoffing at the law and at decency! Who among your posse will be next, Mr. Smith? You? Marshal Ryerson? Two days, first light."

Spunky shook his head. "I guess I got no choice."

"That, quite naturally, Mr. Smith, is up to you."

A very troubled Spunky Smith bought himself two more nights at the boardinghouse, a time that turned into unending torture and frustration. He seriously considered riding away and forgetting the whole thing —Bertha Maguire, Cole Ryerson, others on the posse, the Timberlodge, everything. Life for him spun into a constant battle of decisions discarded and then reconsidered. He feared facing Cole Ryerson's wrath; then his conscience would not let him allow Bertha Maguire to venture alone into the maw of a heinous monster like Bad-Face Ike. Time and again he reasoned that her welfare and her virtue were at stake; their preservation had somehow become his responsibility. Additionally, Ike could capture and use her to get at Cole Ryerson and finally accomplish his fiendish threats.

When daylight pried open Spunky's eyelids on his third morning in Fort Walker, he would rather have faced a cocked six-gun Colt or a hangman's noose.

Grudgingly and reluctantly in his room, he folded

his cleaner clothes back into his war bag and climbed into his grimy trail outfit. At the livery stable, Old Stockholder pranced and pawed in eagerness to be back on the trail after three days of leisure, corn, and grain; Spunky resented the mare's enthusiasm and shared none of it.

So he rode out, awash with anxiety. In the dawn's early light, Bertha Maguire, familiar in the slouch hat with downturned brim and tawny trail coat with upturned corduroy collar, awaited him at Cactus Jack's proper narrow board sidewalk and picket fence. Of the two draft horses that had hauled her buckboard into their desert camp days before, one was saddled.

The other was rigged with a wooden-tree sawbuck packsaddle that appeared properly loaded with bedroll, pots and pans and all manner of packed provisions.

The sublime and the ridiculous continued their combat in Spunky Smith's head.

9

Spunky's strength and assurance flowed back on the approach to Timberlodge. At a high point on the trail to Roughneck Pass Road when they paused to rest the horses, Spunky sighted across a breathtaking panorama of timbered ridges that flowed from the enchanting blue-green of the nearby trees to almost a deep purple darkness away off at the line where land met sky.

"Beautiful to behold, isn't it, Miz Maguire?"

In two days on the trail he'd grown more comfortable with the woman.

"Inspiring," she said.

"Something about it. I always feel stronger in country like this. Is it that hills and mountains are mightier land than out on the flats? Or is it because trees are so much more thick and so powerful looking than sage and creosote bush? The air has more strength in it, too."

"I will lift up mine eyes unto the hills, from whence cometh my help."

"Oh, that's mighty pretty, Miz Maguire. Mighty pretty indeed!"

"Hundred and Twenty-first Psalm."

"Hits the nail square on the head, that's for sure."

Two hours later, close to noon, Spunky spied Dave Nesler's corner claim marker, his rock cairn on Roughneck Pass Road.

The strength he found on Timberlodge was small consolation now. His knees turned rubbery and his heart sank. In mere minutes he'd be face to face with Cole Ryerson, who was sure to be angry over Spunky's disobedience and tardiness. He blanched at the very thought of facing that blistering squint of disapproval.

What was even more blood-chilling was that Cole would be furious that Spunky had allowed the woman to talk him into coming along.

He'd pondered it time and again on their ride out; most of the misfortunes of his life happened in towns. This was just another one of them; such thoughts, however, did little to ease his anxieties.

While they were still some distance from Nesler's cabin, Hans Seabring, carrying his gleaming Sharps, materialized out of the trees that pressed in on both sides of Nesler's trail. He wore his familiar thin straw hat and his long tan duster. At first glance, his pinched-up scientist's face with its tiny oval window-panes clamped to his nose made him appear like some inquisitive little rodent popping out of a hollow log.

"Spunky!" the astronomer called. "Cole will glad be you're back. We've dreadfully worried been. And

Mrs. Maguire. So pleasant again to see you, but I'm so desperately sorry for your loss." Seabring brought thumb and forefinger to bear on his hat brim in a gesture that passed for hat-tipping. Spunky was surprised that Seabring didn't seem surprised to see her.

Bertha looked at Spunky helplessly; she'd forgotten.

"Oh, it's our good doctor, Dr. Hans Seabring," Spunky informed her softly.

Now Bertha put on a benign expression of acknowledgment. "Good day, Doctor," she said pleasantly. "How good to see you again. And thank you for your concern. I so appreciated Marshal Ryerson's sending Mr. Smith to inform me and be with me in my hour of need." Spunky figured that last part was a lie.

Seabring moved out of the fringe of trees and ventured closer to them on the narrow trail leading to Nesler's. He looked sympathetically and almost apologetically at the widow for getting right to the business at hand in the face of Mrs. Maguire's recent tragedy.

"Cole will tell you all that's happened, Spunky. We have Bad-Face Ike's camp found, but still it is like, he says, a standoff. We don't think Ike knows we've found him. Fernando finally scouted him out. Cole's a little . . . well, out of sorts. Complains of being understaffed. He waits before attacking till you get back. For you he's watched for three days and become impatient."

Spunky felt himself slumping lower in the saddle. I didn't need that, Hans, he thought. He turned to Bertha. "We'd best get up there, make our explanations, and get on with things."

"Fernando and I walk around the perimeter patrol to make sure we're not surprised," Seabring added.

"Cole and Cap at the cabin work out logistics of a capture."

"See you in camp, Doc," Spunky called, nudging Old Stockholder. Bertha's horses were in motion at the sam. moment.

Ryerso. heard them coming and was several steps outside the cabin door, legs spread, fists grinding into his hips; even at some distance Spunky felt Ryerson's glare burning into his soul as the horses labored up the forested slope to the cabin, the clop of their hoofs resounding in the heavy silence.

"Mrs. Maguire, good day to you," Ryerson said in hasty acknowledgment. "My sincere condolences on such tragic news. But you weren't expected. Your traveling companion was . . . two days ago! Mr. Smith, is there some resonable explanation?"

Bertha spoke up. "You'll not blame Mr. Smith, Cole. It was I insisted he wait until I could get ready to accompany him on his return. Mark that I do not come in a mourning dress of black bombazine. I prefer to deal with grief differently."

"The degree of your inner strength never ceases to amaze me, Bertha. Besides, mourning clothes would be inappropriate for the trail. However, Mr. Smith's instructions did not give him leave to bring you back." Ryerson, Spunky thought, could get awful formal-sounding when he was on the peck.

"In his defense, he protested strongly."

"I'm sorry, Bertha. We buried John nearly a week ago. Had to. In my mind it would have been totally improper to transport his remains for proper services and burial in Fort Walker."

"And I would have concurred, Cole. Your displeasure with us is warranted and I apologize again. Meanwhile, have I your leave to dismount?"

"Yes. Forgive me. These are not the most pleasant and genial of times and places. A man tends to forget propriety."

Spunky and Bertha secured their horses at a hitch rail near the cabin's front door. Ryerson preceded them, holding the door for Bertha, but turning his back before Spunky entered. Clearly, Spunky thought, Ryerson would take his own good time finding understanding and forgiveness.

The air was cooler but stale inside the cabin's darkness. In the wan light he saw Cap Donovan perched on a short bench at Nesler's modest table. Spunky felt his breathing tighten; it was either that he was waiting for Cole Ryerson's vengeful hammer to fall or indeed it was true that trapped air got thinner the more it was used by inhabitants. Cap jumped up without a word and indicated that Mrs. Maguire should take the only proper seat in the cabin. Wisely, Cap held his tongue; from the look on Ryerson's face, it was clearly his show.

"Bertha, I'm a bit perplexed that you rode all the way out here with Spunky . . . ah, Mr. Smith. It avails little, and the delay has stymied our efforts for several days now, particularly since I have the little devil and his whelps virtually within my grasp!"

"There's an understandable reason, if I can explain, Cole," Bertha began.

Ryerson acted as though he hadn't heard. "It hands me another dandy dilemma, that of now having to release someone to ensure your safe return to Fort Walker."

She turned feisty. And direct. "I have no intention of returning until Bad-Face Ike and his confederates are securely manacled and in your custody."

"That's quite impossible, Bertha. This is man's work, and we must be free of all hindrances. Surely you understand that you'll just have to go back."

"Mr. Ryerson! I explained myself to Mr. Smith, and the fact that he waited two days and accompanied me is proof that he understood. That foul outlaw has deprived me of my means of support in this world and my life's beloved companion. I thought perhaps you knew me better than to think I'd sit home wringing my hands until this matter is brought to a swift conclusion."

"Well, Bertha, I did credit you with better judgment."

"Judgment is what this is all about! The judgment of Bad-Face Ike for the cold-blooded murder of John Jacob Maguire! And I'll not rest until he is in chains."

"Nor will I, Bertha."

"So we're in accord, Cole. Apart from that, I recognize our differences. I'll not get in the way nor hinder your plans or your progress. I've brought ample provisions, and I'll fix three good meals a day for your posse, and it will be a great deal better than the salt pork, jerky, beans, and corn pone of your usual camp fare. But, Marshal Ryerson, in light of what has been taken from me, my place is here, doing everything in my power to assist in the capture of that outlaw Bodene."

"Tempting. And if I forbid it?"

"I'll ask for my husband's weapons and ammunition."

"And?"

Bertha looked Ryerson square in the eye. "I'll take my provisions and embark on my own to confront John's killer."

"You wouldn't!"

Cap and Spunky looked at each other helplessly.

Bertha's chin jutted at an arrogant angle. "Turn me out and see."

To Spunky Smith, at that moment Cole Ryerson hit the most magnificent stride of his entire law-keeping life.

"Then, by the saints," Ryerson proclaimed loudly, the sparks fairly darting from his wide-open eyes, "I'll see you in iron restraints, madam, and sent back to Fort Walker. I'll assign a man to guard and keep you there! It will gravely weaken my force up here, but, by thunder, if that's what it takes, my will be done!"

In spite of herself, Bertha repeated Ryerson's recent words, adding one of her own, "You wouldn't dare!"

Ryerson again punched his fists into his hips in adamant resolve. "Oh, yes, I would!"

Bertha now stood up, stiffened with determination. She planted her spread feet and turned a glare on Marshal Ryerson that equaled his scorching stare glower for glower, her body arrogantly thrust forward as with gritted teeth and pursed lips she, too, faced her most irresistible force in a lifetime of getting immovable objects out of her road by feminine wiles or by sheer weight of will and determination.

"Cole Ryerson, you'll not deprive me of the satisfaction of bringing down the wrath of God upon the head of Ike Bodene for the depraved murder of my husband!"

"Am I to conclude then, madam, that you are the personally appointed emissary of Himself, the Almighty God?"

"If that's how you choose to interpret it, Cole Ryerson . . . *yes!*"

With her words, Ryerson prepared to unleash his final salvo. Spunky stood in awe of being privy to one of the mightiest man-woman debates perhaps in the history of mankind. As Spunky watched in Dave Nesler's humble cottage in the enchanting Timberlodge hills, Ryerson reared back and gathered his supreme force, his broad shoulders squared, his magnificent squint of resolve sparking in his eyes brought to its finest hour and highest need.

"Mrs. Maguire, don't think I haven't had to deal before with women with your level of grit. And, to your eternal credit, you have been blessed with more than your share. Any other woman I would not dare to speak to as harshly so soon after her husband's death. On two memorable occasions I was confronted with plucky women whose desperate circumstances compelled me to take them along on very hazardous missions in the wilderness. I became, by the way, uncommonly fond of both of them, a feeling they returned, each in her very own special way. One of them, a woman named Ruby, didn't survive the harrowing dangers we faced. The other one did, but only after being grievously threatened; she—a woman named Kate—and I married and lived happily for five years until her untimely death."

Bertha Maguire's voice was edged with sarcasm, her patience at a low ebb. "And the point of your sermon, Reverend Ryerson?"

"I'll not make that mistake again. Permission denied, Mrs. Maguire. You're going back to town!"

Bertha pivoted angrily and, seeing the cabin's only window close by, strode to it and, cradling her ample breasts in her crossed arms, stared out at the encircling forest of Timberlodge, her seething fury evident in every line and angle of her body.

Cap Donovan's voice knifed into the leaden silence. "Cole, Hans and Fernando aren't here, and I've not consulted with Spunky yonder. But we've all been together long enough that I think by now I could speak for them."

Wondering at the meaning—and the impudence—of Donovan's intrusion, Ryerson turned his head and squinted again, this time in Cap's direction.

"Hasn't it occurred to you that you might—just might—be making more of this than is necessary? Mrs. Maguire might be guilty of the same. Maybe both of you need to back off a few steps and look at all this from a bit of distance."

Bertha turned away from the window, still hugging herself, but her expression and her anger-stiffened posture softened.

"I'm hearing you out," Ryerson muttered.

"Mrs. Maguire is no flibbertigibbet. With her husband dead at the hands of Bodene or one of his *cabrones,* she was aware of the risks involved in the stand she's taken. In facing up to you, she's indicated that the risk is worth the taking to see Ike brought to justice. She's already expressed her willingness and intention to cook for us. Having twice enjoyed the creations of her culinary genius—once under the strained circumstances of the great American desert

—and then maybe ten times that many experiences with the dismal level of trail rations dished up on this expedition, I think Mrs. Maguire would be a splendid addition to this *posse comitatus.*"

Bertha move closer now to Donovan and Ryerson, her arms relaxed, hands thrust into the pockets of her trail coat as she eagerly watched and listened to Cap. Spunky could see that both Bertha and Ryerson hung on every syllable of Cap's calm voice of reason.

"There's another plus, Cole." Ryerson purposely didn't respond as Cap paused. "Think what good grub will do for the morale of this unit. One of the blessed ties that bind has always been good food. I ask only that you think about it, Cole."

"All right," Ryerson said with a sigh. "I grant there's merit in your argument, Cap." He almost growled it. "I've always tried to be considerate of the feelings and opinions of my deputies. How say you, Spunky?"

Spunky looked at Ryerson wide-eyed. So far, Ryerson hadn't so much as acknowledged he was in the room. "Sounds fine to me." He spoke apprehensively, still unsure of Ryerson's attitude.

"Hans and Fernando are bound to side with you fellas, so it looks like I'm outvoted. More than that, Cap, you come up with some pretty persuasive arguments, points I hadn't thought of. Course I never took any awards for bein' smart. Let me put it this way, Bertha, does Cap's proposition square with you—bein' cook, camp kicker, and mother hen to this rabble of witless scoundrels?"

"If it will hasten bringing the killers of John Maguire to justice, I'll stand on my head if that's what it takes, Cole." Bertha's eyes, Spunky noted, were bright and her smile stretched nearly ear to ear.

"Well, I suppose there could be worse things. We could be stuck with Spunky doing all the cooking. All right, Bertha, every man on this *posse comitatus* has taken the oath as a deputy federal marshal. I'll expect the same of you."

Bertha stood taller and again squarely faced Cole Ryerson, this time her expression beaming. "Ready when you are, marshal," she said.

"Therefore," Ryerson began, "by the authority vested in me as marshal of this federal jurisdiction, raise your right hand and repeat after me . . ."

10

---◆---

"You suppose Dave Nesler'll wander back one of these days soon?" Spunky asked of nobody in particular late in the afternoon of Bertha Maguire's swearing-in as a deputy U.S. marshal up on Timberlodge. Bertha spent the hours between unloading and arranging her "provisions" in Nesler's cabin. She had also given the place a modest cleaning, telling Spunky that—considerately—she'd not clean "that much" since she found herself essentially a guest in someone else's home.

To clean the place to her satisfaction, she told Spunky, would be "improper."

"Dave'll show up any day now," Ryerson answered from what had become his "throne" on the fallen tree a few steps away from the cabin at the fringes of the Timberlodge trees. "I'm surprised you didn't see him in town, Spunky," Cole continued.

The others perched on rocks, stumps, or elsewhere along Ryerson's log. While they waited for the first of

Bertha's "glorious chuck," as one of them had appropriately put it, they lounged with their drinks as the fading sun created deep shadows and pleasant zephyrs around Nesler's cabin clearing. Fernando, who claimed to have no taste for gringo bourbon, had volunteered to walk the guard line among the trees so that Ryerson's Renegades could relax over their drinks.

"I didn't make it a point to get out and around Fort Walker that much that I might have seen him," Spunky replied. "It wasn't what you'd call the best of times."

"How'd she take it, Spunky?" asked Cap Donovan, perched on a rock, swirling his bourbon and branch water mixed with about equal parts; it made a tolerably good drink that appealed to most of Ryerson's Renegades.

Ryerson regarded Cap solemnly. "I hope, oh, Captain, my Captain, that you refer to Mrs. Maguire's reaction to the grim news about Cactus Jack and not some seamy reference to one of those soiled doves that hangs around down at McCurdy's Saloon and how she took it!" All at once, though on the verge of a chuckle at his sly joke, Ryerson looked around apprehensively. To Spunky, Ryerson's often-glaring eyes that had seen so much action this day, looked a bit glazed. "By the way," Ryerson continued, his voice softer now, "where is Cleopatra?"

"Cleopatra?" Spunky asked. "You mean Bertha?"

"Well, don't she behave kind of snooty sometimes like the queen of the Nile to you, Spunk?" Ryerson asked. Fully relaxed and at ease now, the big marshal had another hefty swig from his porcelain cup of old

Group Tightener. Ryerson was fiercely protective of his thick china cup—having his morning eye-opener coffee and his end-of-the-day spirited refreshment out of it. No one else dared touch it.

After years of foolishly burning his lips with hot coffee from an enameled metal cup, he'd confided once to Spunky, he wised up, and his cup of thick porcelain quickly earned a special place in his esteem.

"You said yourself that Bertha's very thorough. Some folks might take that as uppity," Spunky responded, realizing he was getting unusually talkative. "I guess she thinks that cleanliness is next to godliness. Me, now, I guess I ain't that particular, but I don't care to live with the hogs, neither. Cole, I showed her the place over at the brook yonder where Nesler'd scooped out his bathtub. Oh, I saw a little white button down in the bottom." He grinned. "I guess I figured out how ol' Dave takes a bath and washes his underwear at the same time. Bertha's over there 'bathing' before fixing our supper."

Ryerson grunted over another long sip from his cup. "Well, her grub better be superior. I hope you boys know what you're doin', signin' Cleopatra on to tend camp for this outfit."

Spunky realized that Ryerson, bullheadedly, hadn't fully resigned himself to the decision about letting the woman stay.

Dr. Seabring, his eyes glassy behind his little nose-clamped specs, abruptly arose, shoulders back a bit boldly for a man of his retiring nature; he swayed, and Spunky grinned. The doctor, true to Ryerson's word, was made of stern stuff; he'd been into the afternoon grain-squeezin's as eagerly—by appearances maybe more so—as the others. Seabring yanked off his pince-nez and professorially clutched the lapel of his long tan duster in the same motion. He threw back his head as though projecting to the classroom. His loud voice was thick, his words slurred and lispy.

"Cleopatra peris'ed most miserably from the stinging asper-sions of venomous, abstemious asps!"

At the same moment, his comical little low-crowned straw hat spun away from him like a sailed plate; the forest resounded again with the awful thundering roar it had known the fearful night of Cactus Jack's death. The soul-jarring concussion registered with double strength on men who had imprudently dropped their guard and let themselves get soggy with hootch.

Cups dumped their contents and heroics took a holiday as Ryerson's Renegades—including the very surprised but unhurt Dr. Seabring—dove for the nearest cover, most of them against Ryerson's fallen log on the side opposite the woods. Spunky found himself riveted to the Timberlodge gravel and against the log's decaying bark, face-to-face with Cap Donovan.

"What the hell, Cap?" he whispered.

"Keep your head down. Where's your weapon?"

"In the cabin, same as yours."

"He's got us where the sun don't shine, Spunky."

"Bad-Face Ike?"

"I don't mean John Wilkes Booth!"

A shout caromed from out of the forest, chilling and ghostlike. *"Ryer-son!"* There was a hollow, clinging depth to it, perhaps because of some strange sound-bending quality of the trees; the name wafted eerily to Spunky as from some great mysterious distance, heavy and forbidding as a sepulchral call from the grave. Spunky's spine tingled and his neck hairs bristled.

He couldn't see Cole but heard his response.

"Ike? That you?" Ryerson's voice, raised to reach into the woods, was level, fearless.

The caller's voice was nearer now and more natural. "I got your greaser guard with a cocked Colt aimed between his ears."

"That's a hot one, Ike," Ryerson responded, his voice muffled against his protective log, and Spunky shuddered at his audacity. "A greaser calling a greaser a greaser," Ryerson yelled arrogantly.

"You keep smartin' off, Marshal, and this one's dead chili meat!"

"Ah, don't do that, Ike. You got no quarrel with Fernando. Matter of fact, why don't we just send 'em all home, both sides, and you and me go at it out here in the open, Bowies or tooth and claw, to the death, *degüello,* you name your poison, Ike!"

"It's a good bluff, Ryerson, but I got a royal flush. You'll not let this man be killed for the sake of your own miserable hide. I'm comin' in."

"So you don't want a man-to-man fight. It's a free country. Come on in. I got nothin' to stop you, Ike," Ryerson called.

From his low vantage point, a shaken Spunky Smith stared wide-eyed as hard-edged looking *hombres,* armed to the teeth, swarmed out of the shadowy woods around them. At the apex of a ragged, menacing half circle all but surrounding the cabin's rear clearing, one man had Fernando's arm painfully wrenched up behind his back; the same outlaw held the muzzle of an excessively long-barreled Colt against the bone behind Fernando's ear.

Fernando's eyes were big as bowls in fear, his face ashen and pinched in humiliation and pain; his body was bent in defeat and the agony of his cruelly twisted arm.

Beside them and a few steps ahead of the others, leering broadly in gloating superiority stood perhaps the ugliest man Spunky had ever seen. His face was seamed and wrinkled like an overdried prune, lines and furrows crisscrossed. Even at the distance, he saw the heavy pocking that gave him his name and his fame—Bad-Face Ike.

Ike's band, knowing they had the drop on Ryerson's Renegades, eased in closer until they'd formed a wide circle around the five men. Ryerson rose up, considerably sobered.

Beside him, Doc, Cap, and Spunky got to their feet apprehensively, studying the ring of grim-faced enemies, wondering what manner of evil lay in store.

Ryerson looked around at his Renegades; not one had so much as a six-gun buckled on. His guard, Fernando, was clearly out of action.

"I believe you have me at a bit of a disadvantage, Ike," Ryerson confessed, humiliated but perhaps not defeated . . . yet.

Bodene moved closer to Ryerson, chuckling evilly. "A gross understatement, Ryerson. I have your nuts in a vise." He growled it with sinister inflection. As billed, Ike was a short and dark man, stocky with the dusky skin and straight and coarse black hair generally associated with Mexicans or half-breed Indians. Paradoxically, his English had virtually no accent.

"So what's your next move, Ike?" Ryerson asked, his voice surprisingly level. Spunky's heart swelled in admiration of Ryerson. He was as calm as though he were arranging a horse swap; Spunky knew Bodene's evil intentions.

"You got my note, Ryerson?"

Ryerson tapped his chest. "I carry it. Right here. I read it over every once in a while. Inspires me to run to earth and hang the egg-suckin' son of a bitch that wrote it!"

Ike grinned, an oily and evil smirk. "You're a dead man."

Ryerson spoke resolutely. "I guess so. But before I go, I must inform you that you are under arrest for jailbreak, for train robbery, and for the cold-blooded murder of John Jacob Maguire. You'll hang, Ike, whether it's me that gets you or not. The law will hound you till they drop your gallows trap."

"A lot of good all that talk does you out here, *amigo.*" As Bad-Face Ike laughed sardonically at a soon-to-be-dead man's arrogance, Ryerson's treasured thick porcelain mug, which had fallen when he leaped for cover moments before and now lay in the dirt a short distance from his feet, explosively disintegrated in a shower of sharp white shards and pulverized gravel and dust as the air was rent again with the belching concussion of a big-caliber rifle speaking out from the trees on the slopes above the cabin clearing.

The eyes of the five Ryerson's Renegades and those of about a dozen and a half of Bodene's men darted in the direction the bullet had come from.

As they stared transfixed, Bertha Maguire strode resolutely out of the forest gripping Cactus Jack's powerfully breeched, short-barreled 1873 Winchester saddle-ring carbine that threw a man-stopping bullet from its peppy .44/40 cartridge. Shoeless, her damp feet were brownly moccasined with decomposed granite and pine needles. Her sodden chemise of a durable muslin material—edged, breastline and hem, with attractively designed tatting—put on in modesty for her swim, conformed to every feminine curve and swell of her capable, attractive body.

Bertha's dark hair, still drenched from her bath, was pasted to her head and hung, clung, and dripped in unattractive strands and tendrils around her ears and forehead.

As the eyes of nearly two dozen men took in this comely apparition from out of the woods, her voice boomed with unexpected authority.

"Ike Bodene! Back away!" With her words came the sinister, mechanical chattering cadence of the spent case ejecting and a deadly gleaming gray lead-tipped brass round aligning itself with cold precision into the breech. "My late husband's rifle is sighted in higher than I realized. And probably at a hundred yards, and I am at fifty. I intended to shoot off only the cup handle of Marshal Ryerson's favorite mug. I believe that I have the range, the windage, the elevation, and other variables compensated for. So, Bad-Face Ike, if you will turn a few degrees sidewise of me, damn you, sir, I'll blow your nose for you, and you'll have something else to disfigure your hideous countenance!"

More resembling an adolescent girl ready for bed in her nightie than a vengeful widow, Bertha began an ominously slow, barefoot stalk in her wet, clinging chemise down the untimbered slope toward the cabin. All the while, the carbine's half-moon butt plate was nestled against her shoulder socket, her open right eye aligned with hind and front sight directly targeted on Bodene's nose, muzzle weaving but unerringly centered as though gimbal-governed. "Otherwise," she proclaimed as she neared the circle of men—friend and foe—staring at her dumbfounded, "I have but to compensate a fraction of a degree vertical or horizontal and, sir, your ugly face will be history just as you destroyed the handsome, virile features for all time of my provider and lover, John Jacob Maguire!" Bertha's voice rose up an emphatic octave in pitch. "Make me the instrument of Thy divine judgment, O Lord!"

Ike's eyes darted, and his head swiveled in bewilderment, his mind in obvious turmoil. Fernando's captor was equally confused and fearful of the shrieking vixen with the unerring Winchester; his grip on Fernando's wrenched arm relaxed as his resolution wavered.

Ike watched helplessly as Fernando straightened, his near hand coming up cupped to scornfully nudge the long Colt barrel away from his head like a man shooing off an ear-invading fly. In one smooth and deft motion of arm and body, he twisted the gun from his captor's hand by the barrel, flung it to twirl into the air, leaped and spun in a graceful balletlike pirouette, made a smooth catch of the gun's grip coming down, and catlike hit the ground in a perfect gunfighter's crouch with the cocked Colt covering Bodene's solar plexus.

Spunky wanted to cheer.

"The disadvantage has changed sides, Ike," Ryerson growled. "The little lady or the greaser will level the first man who makes a wrong move!"

Bodene's eyes narrowed. "We still got more guns than you. When the shooting starts, you're all chili meat."

"But you won't know that, Ike, for you'll be the first dead!"

"We'll see about that, Ryerson."

"I will see about that, Ike!" His head pivoted. "Bertha!" he screamed back over his shoulder. "You heard this shrivel-faced bastard! Now's the time to avenge your man and be the instrument of God's vengeance all at once. Shoot the son of a bitch!"

The woman's voice from behind him came clearly but calm and infallible. "I'll not stoop to his brand of cowardice and abomination. They must fire the first shot!"

Ryerson's reaction came like quicksilver; he edged closer to Bodene, ready to goad him to rash action. Spunky quivered with emotion; he'd never seen Boot Hill Cole's face so tight, even in the most danger-fraught challenges. Cole was consumed with outrage to his very depths. "Then there's the other way to bring this to a head, goddammit! All right, Ike. I grant you your wish. Maybe you won't get to cut me up in little pieces and feed me to the dogs while I watch as I bleed to death. But we're down to cases here, and you're heeled and I ain't. So go ahead. Haul out your iron and blaze away, and we'll go slidin' down the chutes into hell together! One or the other of my Renegades'll level you the second your firing pin pricks the bullet's primer!"

Ike hesitated, his eyes scant inches from Ryerson's.

"Go get heeled, Ryerson. I'll face you over six-guns."

"Bullshit! I offered you that option, and you ignored it. You wanted me in your clutches, dammit, and here I am! You know damned well that if you win a straight-across six-gun showdown, Fernando or Bertha won't shoot you for being fastest. They ain't backshooters. They'll let you ride out of here. Unless you cheat, and this time you won't dare. You're home free. But shoot me down unarmed and *you're* dead chili meat." Ryerson edged boldly closer. "So that's the way it'll be, Ike. Shoot me and die, or stick out your hands for the manacles and live until the hangman adjusts the hemp. It's your choice."

"What about my men?"

"You care about that slime!? When did your heart turn soft, Ike? Well, the very best they can expect is accessory before and after the fact of the cold-blooded murder in the death of John Maguire. There must be other possible indictments for any and all, so they're good for a long stretches in Yuma or Leavenworth if they don't hang with you. No deals for them or you. Like you, they made the choice to ride outside the law. *Degüello,* remember, Ike, no quarter given, no survivors."

"But there can be. I still got a lot of the Southern and Central loot, Cole. How's about a deal?"

Spunky hoped he could remember Ryerson's response to tell his grandkids—it was that good.

"Yeah, hand it over to me for a return to the authorities. Your cooperation may get you roast beef instead of chicken the day of your hangin'. I've been known to make deals, sometimes beyond the bounds of my authority. But justice profited. Even if I was down to my last cigarette, I'd make no deals with the likes of you. Me and these *hombres* of mine here, and the little lady yonder, well, our integrity ain't for sale. We stand for somethin' you wouldn't know about: We're stouthearted men . . . and woman! Now that you know where we stand, what'll it be, Ike? Guns blazin' or your Colt butt forward—and none of your stupid road-agent spin, neither. Bertha or Fernando'll kill you just as dead. Tell your men to drop their guns and stick out your hands for the shackles."

Bodene bobbed his head. He'd come in with all the cards in his favor and now was cold decked. "I got no choice?"

"Nary a one, Ike."

"God damn that woman."

"Cleopatra? Huh-uh. God *bless* 'er!"

11

---◆---

Well, Ike," Ryerson said a few minutes later, "looks like you get the first-class treatment. I only had one set of iron handcuffs to bring along." With that, he snapped them on the outlaw's wrists. "The rest of your boys'll have to be content with getting their wrists roped. And since we got to watch all of you like a hawk, and short-handed at that, I brought along enough light hemp to hitch you all together around the neck. Wove together like a daisy chain. That ought to keep things fairly serene. Again you get the best treatment. I'll put you at the head of the line. That way you won't have to have your nose right behind some jasper likely to cut a big fart. I think the boss should always have the exalted position."

Bodene, standing with Ryerson away from his outlaw band, glowered wordlessly.

Bertha had gone back to fetch her things at the brook and then to see what could be done to feed the hands as well as their unwelcome guests; she only grumbled over the extra mouths to feed because of who they were and that they had no mess gear.

Under Cap's command, Spunky, Dr. Seabring, and Fernando rounded up Bad-Face Ike's outlaws, herded them together, and milled them into a circle before settling them in comfortable bedding ground. Taking equally spaced points in the ring, they walked the perimeter like night guards on a cattle drive.

"Puts me in mind of going up the Texas Trail with a couple thousand head in the summer of '79," Cap said.

"Believe I'd rather manage that many snarly, muley longhorns than this bunch," Spunky said.

"Almost be a toss-up," Cap replied.

"All I ask," Spunky said, "is that you don't start singin' 'The Streets of Laredo' like you was ridin' herd at night."

"Ike," Ryerson went on several steps away with the outlaw leader, "despite of, but in light of, our bad blood, there's gonna be some real problems in logistics in gettin' all of you back to Fort Walker. First off, it's gonna be miserable for you tonight. It's getting on to dark. It's turnin' chilly, and I won't be able to send any men over to your camp for your bedrolls and gear. You'll have to be content with the discomfort till in the mornin'."

Bodene continued the silent treatment.

"But we can go out and bring in your horses, get 'em unsaddled and watered and grained and give 'em some oats if you tell me where you left 'em before your invasion."

Ryerson looked at Ike who now watched him strangely. "What's the matter?" Ryerson asked.

Ike looked down at his handcuffed wrists.

"What the hell's wrong, Ike?"

Ike's head still hung. "We walked over here."

"You what!?"

"We figured to kill you all to get your mounts so we could round 'em up. I didn't know about that woman bein' here."

"Well, I'm a sunbeam! You want to tell me just what the hell happened?"

"Night before last. My nighthawk was drunk. Went to sleep. The picket line got undone and they just wandered off. We tried to hunt for 'em, but they'd got too far. They just got halters on, so they can eat and drink so they'll survive."

"You don't have a single horse?"

Ike again studied his manacles. He shook his head sheepishly.

"Under other circumstances, I'd be bent over laughin' just now, Ike. What it is, though, is a damned pesky logistical pain, which is something you outlaw jaspers never have to think about the man tracking you down. And right there's one of the major differences in our occupations. Your only concern is to shoot us down like a dog, and maybe take our horse, our guns, and our gear for what it's all worth. The lawman, now, he's got to consider transporting a prisoner clear back to town, even if it's a hundred miles, and the suspect's welfare and chuck in transit. Else there's a big complaint to the presiding judge by some pipsqueak lawyer and maybe a mistrial 'cause you been abused, and I'm suspected of sadism. If a lawman's hauling in a dead fugitive—the only way to prove it for bounty, reward, or in a court of law—it may be a hundred miles and a hundred and ten in the shade, and if you don't think that don't give a lawman the fantods, just try it some time. I believe that's why they took to taking in only heads in gunnysacks. That method keeps down the bugs and the wiggle worms that'll infest a dead body on the trail. And a gawdam almighty righteous stink, too. All kind of gruesome, but that's our job."

"It ain't like I planned it, Ryerson."

"Your horses are gone?"

"You think I'm making this up?"

"In your best interests, I hope not, Ike. Just now, I'll get you over with your ring and a dally around your neck. It's two rough days by horse to Fort Walker. Afoot in this heat the past few days . . . I don't know. I purely don't know. I got to do something, and I don't relish the mess you got me into. But now you've gone and murdered a man that I got pretty persuasive evidence of. This one I can positively prove. So you'll hang and finally be out of my life forever. No more jailbreaks for me to come chasin' you all over the nation for."

At daybreak Ryerson dispatched Cap and Fernando with three horses with wood sawbuck packsaddles and panniers to round up the outlaws' gear at their camp. At that, he figured the best he could get away with was their bedrolls, war bags, and mess kits. Their saddles and most of their camp gear would have to be sacrificed.

"And watch your step and mind your back trail," he warned them sternly as he looked up at the mounted pair, two of his beloved friends. "I don't need to lose any more deputies, and I don't need to lose any more good friends!"

One at a time, he looked Cap and Fernando straight in the eye to reinforce his meaning.

"Now, I put nothin' past that sneaky bastard. Be just like him to've dropped off a couple of bushwhackers along the way out there to dry-gulch just such a patrol as this."

Ryerson paused again. "I tell you, boys, I'm about at my wit's end. If anything was to happen to you two, and me left with Bertha and Spunky and Hans to take them in afoot over maybe sixty miles of bakin' desert, I'm afraid I'd be pretty hard put. So, dammit, get back here in one piece!"

The waning afternoon sun again painted long shadows of the majestic pines, and the cooling murmurs had begun in their topmost branches before Cap and Fernando led their pack train back with what necessities of Ike's camp they could load on the horses. He assigned Doc Seabring the responsibility of "offloading" and distributing pieces of personal gear among the prisoners. Their wrist and neck restraints kept them properly fettered but free enough to deal with their belongings. While Seabring moved among them portioning out their individual packs, Fernando stood guard with his unerring Winchester from a nearby promontory, cautioned by Ryerson within the prisoner's hearing to summarily shoot the first man to make a menacing move.

Meekly respectful of the big and resolute gringo lawman—who would have totally intimidated them separately—Bodene's men claimed their gear and settled down again into their close circle on the ground.

Ryerson held a subdued council of war over Bertha's supper of fresh bread with preserves, smoked ham, and sweet, succulent baked beans and some of the finest camp coffee any of them had ever put lip to.

A few steps away, clustered in a close circle for guarding, Ike's gang members grinned broadly, their deep brown eyes sparkling at their gringo keepers as they scraped, sopped, and wiped every morsel and drop from their plates. Such heavenly chuck was a luxury most of them had never before experienced.

"Cole, something's going to have to be done," Bertha warned as she joined the men in the cabin yard with her plate of food. "I planned provisions for about a week for six people. The first meals I've fixed are for four times that many. I can't keep this up too long."

"I been thinkin' about that. We need fresh meat," Ryerson responded. "And, by the way, Bertha, I take back and apologize for anything said spitefully or in anger yesterday. You have risen to the occasion like a champion, a true Ryerson Renegade, and lest I tread upon your feminine sensibilities, an honorary but first-class, fourteen-karat Stouthearted Man!"

"Here! Here!" Dr. Seabring yelled, and the others, though strangers to Seabring's exclamation, recognized it as unrestrained approval and added their cheers.

"But one thing, madam," Ryerson drawled sternly,

and all eyes were on him, Bertha's in particular. "You killed my porcelain coffee mug," he went on in an accusing tone. "That breach of judgment I'll never forg . . ." He paused dramatically and Bertha's eyes on his were big as bowls. His face suddenly softened. "I'll never forget as long as I live! What a shot! That sure got Ike's attention, and did you see how quickly the lion became a lamb? Magnificent!"

Those around him grinned broadly; Bertha's accurate shot had saved all their lives.

Ryerson turned dead serious, realistic. "Bertha, in the morning, after we get this pack of prisoners on the move, I'll dispatch Fernando out to get us some fresh meat for tomorrow. Based on the logistics of our problem, that of having to take them home afoot, we'll have to run this like a cattle drive. We'll proceed slow, and we'll have to send the cook crew on ahead to establish the noon stop and night camp, get supper, and gear up for breakfast."

All watched Ryerson with rapt interest as he turned a pesky problem into a workable plan.

"Under the circumstances, gentlemen and lady, I'm havin' to deal with things on a step-by-step basis. I try to plan ahead, but decisions may have to be made on a moment's notice. So please bear with what you call the exigencies of the situation. Dr. Seabring, I assign you to Mrs. Maguire as her guard and support associate or colleague, however you want to look upon the assignment."

"Position gratefully accepted," Dr. Seabring said magnanimously. To most men, subservience to a woman was demeaning; Ryerson realized he had chosen well. Hans Seabring's broad education had also given him a broad mind.

"Fernando," Ryerson went on, and the southwesterner's dark but sparkling eyes swung and locked on his acknowledged hero. "You'll be our swing man, scout, and hunter. Bertha's gonna need fresh meat at least every other day, even if you have to ride back into the Timberlodge country for deer. Meantime, you'll ride courier between the two divisions of our drive, keeping both units informed. By the way, *amigo,* I never even saw a darting, hovering hummingbird maneuver as well as you with that fandango you pulled yesterday evening flickin' that long-snouted Colt off your ear and slippin' out of the snare of that *hombre* twistin' your arm. Then I have never seen such a performance of gun-handling and turning the tables as you pulled off right in front of those *cabrones.* I believe, Fernando, that I speak for the rest of Ryerson's Renegades, you—and Bertha—saved us all yesterday evening! Each of you ought to have a medal!"

Fernando accepted Ryerson's words with a grateful, shy smile that brightened his face and showed his clean, well-set teeth. His words were softly spoken and self-conscious, but rich in their simplicity. "For Señor Ryerson, and for his Renegades—Spunky, Cap, Señor Dr. Seabring, *y* Señora Maguire—I would do anything. Die maybe. But this day yesterday I see what I need to do, and I just do it!" Fernando shrugged his left shoulder only in his peculiar self-effacing way, and Ryerson's Renegades hearts swelled. Fernando had proved himself a stouthearted man; love and cohesion

138

of spirit mounted in Ryerson's camp at that moment, and his own heart was stronger.

"All right," Ryerson now said, seeing that the iron was hot enough to strike to bring them out of a misty kind of reverie, "so much for living in the past. We got first-class puzzles to noodle over. Six of us got three times that number of prisoners to get back to Fort Walker hale and hearty to stand trial for a full bill of indictment that includes cold-blooded murder and accessory before and after the fact in the killing of Jack Maguire."

Bertha's soft eyes rested now on Ryerson, the man her husband had idolized. In the look was no romantic connection; her late husband's employer and mentor simply had risen dramatically in her not easily merited esteem. She saw with new light his ability to mold and forge men to achieve greatly and, she noted, he did it with soft, approving words. But when he needed them, his words could be forceful and pointed as sticks.

He paused, looking around him. "Most of us, excepting, of course, Mrs. Maguire and Fernando— coincidentally our saviors on this mission—have been in war and are familiar with the problems and logistics of moving bodies of men great distances for combat. Gentlemen and lady, this situation is comparable, if not more so, and calls for the very best each of us, and as a unit, has to deliver. They are a bunch of scurvy *banditos, comancheros,* and cutthroats that we'd rather see dead, but I insist that each and every one of them—as our responsibility now—is a human being who must arrive in Fort Walker on his feet, clean in body and clothing and well-nourished. That, lady and gentlemen, is your charter and your marching orders. Now, do I hear any questions . . . or arguments?"

Like a schoolboy staying silent until recognized, Cap Donovan raised his hand.

"Cap?"

"Fort Walker the closest place to find 'em mounts?

"I've thought about it. There is a place, a prime place, a lot closer than Fort Walker, but still a hard day's ride."

"Which is?" Cap asked eagerly.

"There's a cavalry cantonment about two miles off the Southern and Central right-of-way east of where we came on to the tracks. The troop used to be stationed at Fort Walker proper right after the war when they worked the so-called Indian menace until the Southern and Central line was put through this far south. Then the War Department, in its infinite wisdom, had 'em establish base closer to the rail line and transfer the post complement down there for ease of maneuvering or mobilizing. Not a fortified type operation in that sense of the word either. It's your run-of-the-mill quadrangle or compound of barracks and stables, officers' quarters and command post, sutler's and farrier's buildings, such as that."

"We could get horses there?" Cap asked, his voice excited.

"Oh, they've always got twenty or thirty broken-down plugs in reserve that don't qualify for service; venerable old warhorses out of harness left to live out their days pasturing and cared for by the grooms, and, like I say, any number of old hacks that might fit in in a pinch as pack animals. They'd do for Bodene's bunch."

"Well, there's your answer, Cole," Cap enthused. "You're a federal officer with an emergency. Couldn't you go over there and requisition enough of those nags to get Ike's gang horsed, and take 'em back later?"

"Sorry to be one jump ahead of you, Cap. Yeah, that idea occurred to me."

"Then let's do it!"

"Hold your horses, Cap. I appreciate your enthusiasm and the level of your reasoning, but the plain truth is I'd need at least two of you with me to wrangle that many cayuses back here. That leaves three to walk guard over Ike's eighteen—ain't good tactical judgment."

"Cole?" Bertha Maguire's voice piped up, questioning. "Any chance you could take a couple of the prisoners to help ride herd. It's in their best interests."

Ryerson studied her, his eyes thoughtful. "Damned good idea, Berty," he said. "The kind of thinking I need. But that one won't scour neither. I'd have to be forever on the alert that they didn't skedaddle the minute my back was turned. That or poke a Mexican hideout stiletto between my back ribs. You know what they say, there ain't no honor among thieves . . . nor cutthroats!"

Ryerson again turned thoughtful, his jaw clamped, looking into the blue sky over the green Timberlodge trees for answers to his quandary. His Renegades were silent, too, each working over the needs and possible solutions.

"Naw," Ryerson said, finally breaking a long silence. "We take 'em in afoot, hands tied and strung together around the neck. Like I originally planned. I don't see any other workable alternatives."

"Wait! Why I did not think of it before?!" Dr. Seabring's voice rose. "Cole! The most important prospect you missed. From the post over there you could get some of the troops to help with the drive back."

Ryerson grinned. "Guess I hadn't given that much thought, Hans. Main hurdle I see there is that Major Locke, the commander over there, is a regular old fussbudget about being understaffed and short-handed. Every time I've been down there all that man has done is whine and sputter about his shortage of manpower and the inability of his superiors, the War Department, and the Congress to keep his installation properly manned."

Ryerson turned reflective. "On the other hand, if I got a little nasty he might cave in. Good prospect, Hans, damned good prospect. I'll work on it. Maybe get this bunch down to the rail line and I could flag a train for a ride over there; probably save me better than a half day. Yeah, distinct possibilities! We'll work toward that, by God!"

Ryerson got up and walked around to ease the cramps from being parked on his log so long. "We'll start our march in the morning. At least get 'em over to the rail line."

Bertha's voice again piped up. "There might be a better way than having their hands and necks tied, Cole."

"You want to elaborate on that one for us, Berty?"

"Pair the prisoners up. Side by side. Tie each pair's

142

near ankles together, almost like a three-legged race at a church picnic. Only give them a little more slack. With practice, they'll learn to walk in unison. Free their hands. Make sure they believe that anyone caught bending over trying to untie the ropes is dead on the spot. I think we'd make better time. They'd feel freer, and maybe more cooperative."

"They wouldn't be able to run," Spunky enthused.

"It's risky. You folks don't know how that Bad-Face Ike's mind works like I do. He's slid like a greased pig out of two jails I know of. That scheme might not work, as good an idea as it is. But I tell you what. We'll give it a whirl in the mornin'. First time it gives us a problem, we go back to roped wrists and Ryerson's daisy chain around their necks!"

Ryerson paused a long time for effect. Spunky remembered the pregnant pauses and the emphatic words of the day of the formation of Ryerson's Renegades in McCurdy's Saloon in Fort Walker. Cole's voice intruded; its gravity reaching deep within each of them and each for varying reasons.

"Ladies and gentlemen, we have been fortunate. Exceeding fortunate to have so easily brought Ike Bodene to bay. Now . . . I want each and every one of you to hold this as your foremost thought through the rest of this goddam cotillion till we get 'em safe at Fort Walker. This Bodene is the slickest, treacherousest throat-cutter since Attila the Hun. We got him and his men for murder. He's desperate and vicious, nothing to lose. Die now or on the Fort Walker gallows, it's all the same to him. Out here he has a chance for freedom, and he'll watch for the holes in our defenses. Ike plays by different rules—the devil's rules—than we do, we who operate from fairness, decency, and the Golden Rule. He knows the weaknesses of gringo sentimentalities. So watch him. Play his game. But by his rules, which is more vicious than cutthroat poker. The only way to survive. He'll give no quarter. *Degüello*. Remember?"

12

The pace down Roughneck Pass Road and off Timberlodge to the desert was agonizingly slow. At the first nooning, out on the flats in the glaring sun, while the long, dusty, fatigued column of trudging captives was still two hundred yards off, Spunky could see Bertha striding up and down impatiently while Hans Seabring stood by as patiently as possible trying to placate her.

Even this far out of earshot, Spunky's mind's ear could hear her sputtering about the food getting cold or being cooked to cardboard. Spunky grinned to himself; Ryerson's plan would take some adjusting and getting used to. But, he also thought, Ryerson's Renegades could—and would—do it.

By late morning of the second day, they had reached the Southern and Central tracks and were headed east along the twin bands of high iron. Spunky remembered a siding a mile or so along the way he'd seen on the ride up. A sluggish spring—probably fed from thawing runoff of Timberlodge snow following a fissure deep in the bedrock—bubbled out of the desert a hundred or so yards north of the track to create a wide, trenchlike slough that required a long culvert under the Southern and Central right-of-way before the brackish trickle lost itself again in the desert's loosely compacted decomposed granite and sand. Cottonwoods had somehow migrated there and propagated, creating a shady oasis in the sprawling, barren but rolling flats that elsewhere sustained little more than juniper, piñon, and chaparral stretching to the horizons as far as the eye could see.

The Southern and Central had laid its rails for a siding here maybe, Spunky mused, for a pleasant but wilderness-bound layover for passenger cars, leaving the main line open, or simply to sidetrack an occasional empty freight car or two; or both possibilities.

As the marching column, guarded and guided by Ryerson's horsemen, approached the slough and the towering, bulking green of the cottonwoods and their welcoming shade, Spunky saw Bertha and Hans Seabring busy fixing the noon dinner in the dim light of the spreading grove, as well as that of a single boxcar standing opposite. It was ideal; cool shadow from two sides with handy squaw wood for a cookfire.

Spunky heard Cole Ryerson, riding point, whoop loudly. Wondering at the cause of Boot Hill Cole's sudden jubilation in the face of constant frustration, irritation, and anxiety, Spunky—closest to the marshal—rode nearer to him as he pivoted in his sweated saddle.

"Whoo-hee, Spunk!" Ryerson exulted, seeing an old pard close by. Ryerson's long front hair was sweat-plastered to his forehead, his face bleached and gaunt by the strain of command and burdensome responsibility. Now he grinned broadly, an expression that crinkled his eyes. Spunky was heartily encouraged.

"I do believe I have just been handed my ace in the hole!" I'm on my way to a flush, a by-God royal stouthearted flush!"

"What're you runnin' off about, Cole?"

"We have flanked cruel fate and shortly will have his works surrounded!"

"I don't get you."

"Why, a surrogate jail, Spunky. It can easily be guarded by three while I take two on a fast reconnaissance patrol to the cavalry post for remounts. Four days hence we'll be in Fort Walker instead of six or seven. And with saddle-weary and not footsore prisoners!"

Ryerson cautioned Spunky to keep silent about his inspiration until after they'd eaten. While Fernando guarded the prisoners who lounged with their after-dinner smokes under the cottonwoods, Ryerson signaled for his Renegades to circle up beside the open door of the Southern and Central boxcar.

"Gather round, folks," he announced happily, his ruddy face already showing the release of strain. "I told you up on Timberlodge that circumstance might dictate our tactics moment to moment. Just such an eventuality has occurred. Here's my plan, and please hear me out before taking issue."

Cap, Spunky, Seabring, and Bertha sprawled in the boxcar's shade while Ryerson strode up and down on the sidetrack's roadbed of gray, pocked slag and cinders before the car door. Spunky's insides felt light with optimism.

"This wheeled edifice behind me comes to us as a boon to our quest. We lock Bodene's bunch up with their bedrolls and what other comforts we can permit them. Three Renegades can guard them. Let out one leashed pair at a time for relief and guard 'em close, and shoot 'em if they try to run."

For effect, Ryerson beamed his most intent look on those surrounding him. They watched attentively. "Fernando and Bertha ride with me. We leave right now and should get to the cavalry post tonight. With any luck, we'll be back tomorrow evenin' with the remounts. Now, Cap, Hans, and Spunky, keep that door closed and have at least one man on watch at all times. Any questions?"

Cap Donovan studied Ryerson for a long moment before speaking. "Cole, Spunky and the doctor and I have a good idea of the needs. Why don't you and the lady and Fernando get fogging. We'll stand good guard. It's our necks at risk."

"Pleased to hear you say that, Cap," Ryerson said. "Strip your horses but keep your rigs handy for a pursuit if you need to. Drop the loads off the pack-horses and organize a good camp. Control our remuda better than Bad-Face Ike did his. I got one other request."

"Which is?" Cap asked.

"Up at the head end of the slough, by the spring. Dig us out a nice bathtub-size pool and then let it settle and clear. When we get back, we'll treat Ike's boys to a cleanup and a shave and wash their duds. Clean up ourselves. That way, we'll ride into Fort

Walker like a trim fightin' unit with well-cared-for prisoners, our heads high. Now, let's get them boys boxcar-incarcerated while Bertha, Fernando, and I tighten cinches. Does everybody understand what he's to do?"

Murmurs of agreement met Ryerson's question.

Years later, Spunky Smith would remember that his first thoughts when it happened were something he'd heard about the best-laid plans of mice and men often going to hell in a handbasket.

The next morning came up blissfully balmy, the sun coasting easily across the sky; a constant soft breeze from somewhere assured a very tolerable temperature, leaning Spunky toward relaxed feelings as he guarded the secured carload of desperadoes, Winchester at the ready. Following Ryerson's orders, Cap and Dr. Seabring were at the head of the slough trying to work a catch basin in the gravel to serve as a cleanup tank for Ryerson's Renegades and their captives.

With no place comfortable to sit on the ground and the iron rail also making a poor seat, Spunky climbed the bolted iron rungs of a ladder at one end of the car. The door was fastened by a great cast-iron hasp, and he could hear murmurs of quiet conversation from the men inside. On top of the car, Spunky sat down on the narrow centered running board, three closely spaced planks bolted to leveling supports to provide a walkway from caboose to engine for members of the train crew.

The sun and the air were serene up here, the view superb from his higher vantage point; he wished he had a telescope or binoculars to better look at his now-beloved Timberlodge. At least he could see its beckoning greenery from here.

Life for Spunky Smith at that moment was utter bliss. The prisoners were secure; he could hear if any of them called for a relief break and be down off the top of the car in three shakes of a lamb's tail. At the moment the solitude was welcome; it had been rare on this trip, and Spunky vowed to enjoy it while it lasted. He carefully laid his Winchester on the planking beside him and rolled a smoke.

As he puffed languidly, Spunky flopped on his side to rest on his elbow and watch the cottonwood leaves quiver in the soft, midmorning breeze. Promptly his pose became uncomfortable for his elbow, and he stretched out on the running board, still clutching a bit less than half of his glowing cigarette between his lips, and began a study of the almost turquoise-colored sky. A few clouds stood glaringly white against the awesome depth of color; Spunky allowed his body and mood to relax and take it all in. He shifted his eyes and his head lazily to study a puff of snowy cloud in the periphery of his vision; under closer scrutiny, it was perfectly shaped to resemble Old Stockholder's rump and tail. Spunky's relaxed, heavy eyelids slid shut.

Up at the head end of the slough, Dr. Seabring stood, thigh-deep in the water of the basin, trousers off, his rump and hips shrouded in short-legged white linen small clothes. Otherwise he wore only a shirt, his small oval glasses and straw hat, its low crown tattered from a bullet's crease. He harkened to an approaching sound.

"Comes a train, Cap," he said. The blend of chuffing, steam, driving rods, and clanking wheels were indistinguishable from the distance, but the train noise was unmistakable.

"Probably the one Cole would've flagged to ride over to the cavalry place. We're almost a day ahead of that schedule, thank God. I hope Spunky's got more sense than to be standing around in the roadbed," Cap said.

While an exhausted Spunky Smith snoozed in deep oblivion, a short and stubby black locomotive, roaring and rolling in reverse, wheezed to a stop a short distance just east of the sidetrack; a man in striped blue bib overalls and soft cap of the same material dropped off the engine, threw a switch, and the engine huffed and puffed backward into the siding.

The engineer, a twelve-year railroading veteran who took exaggerated pride in his work, cased the engine in, the couplers meshing almost imperceptibly, but enough of a gentle nudge to waken Spunky to a hazy reality.

"What the hell was that?" he asked himself aloud, looking around at the sky, half forgetting for the moment even where he was. The blue heavens over him had darkened under dense, drifting locomotive smoke from a huge pear-shaped stack.

The worker on the ground worked the lever locking the couplers with a clank and waved a trainman's highball to the engineer. Spunky grew more alert and aware. "Hey!" he yelled in panic at the top of his lungs. "Wait a minute!" His shout was drowned out by a shriek of expelled hissing steam and massive iron wheels and rims screaming their protest against the slightly curved sidetrack as the locomotive inched forward in jolts and jerks.

The engine, all staccato chugs, clatters, and gnash of driver wheels slipping for traction on the rails, and pistons and driving rods overriding Spunky's shouts of astonishment and appeal, eased out of the siding with its single boxcar in tow.

The crewman again threw the manual switch to align the rails back to the main track and leaped for the sill step up to the engine cab.

The lurch of the engine quickly gathering momentum to head east sent Spunky grabbing for his Winchester as it slipped off the running board beside him and began a clattering slide down the gently sloped roof toward the edge of the boxcar.

"Judas Priest!" Spunky's still-groggy mind rebelled. "What in *the* hell is going on?!" He had turned into a defenseless ant in a world of dense black smoke and grit, rolling acceleration and jolting and swaying, powerless against a malevolent force he had no means to combat. The thought ricocheted through his frenzied, confused mind that perhaps he had died and was on his way down the chutes into hell.

Clutching his Winchester, Spunky—pierced by spikes of unreasoning panic—dropped from a crouch to the narrow planking to cling for dear life; his hat sailed away on a fierce, speeding headwind, bounced twice on the tin roof, and was lost in a shroud of heat and black smoke and soot as the engineer advanced the throttle, and the truncated train leaped to what to Spunky was a breakneck speed.

With the wind howling around him to rip at his face and his hair and clothing and to bring tears to his eyes,

Spunky dared a glance back under the cloak of dense black smoke at the band of cottonwoods marking the slough at right angles to the track as the trees—his last touch with security—quickly slipped from sight in the distance.

"Why me?" his shocked and bewildered mind roared. "Why does everything always happen to *me?!*"

13

Their gravel-lined bathtub complete—Seabring dubbed it "Donovan's Ditch"—the former Texas Ranger captain and his scientist companion cleaned up and relaxed in the pleasant and restful camp they'd created in the cottonwoods. Anticipating Ryerson's return, Doc and Cap had made it into a model of woodscraft.

The site was cleared of brush and weeds, a firepit dug and ringed with rocks, and the area around it cleared of combustibles. They gathered in an abundance of handy dead "squaw wood" from under the trees and broke up and neatly stacked enough to last through several night camps, even though they knew it would probably be but one.

The pair had a dual purpose in amassing their ambitious woodpile; it cleared clutter from under the trees to add to the aesthetics of their attractive, welcoming camp.

Space for six bedrolls around their fire ring was rid

of branches, twigs, and projecting stones that could turn a sleeper's bedroll into a torture rack. The entire sleep site then was raked and swept with a big, leafy cottonwood limb.

Now Cap, his wet hair doused in the stream to rinse off the sweat, and combed and slicked down, sprawled with the gratifying fatigue of a job well done on top of his spread bedroll, his head on his saddle, studying the depth of sky through the cottonwood limbs and leaves. Dr. Seabring had unpacked his telescope and, with appropriate soft cloths, polished the tube and its eyepiece and lens.

"That was a job of work," Cap said, referring to their digging. "I had my eye open for gold but didn't see any. Old Nesler must've found enough to keep his appetite whetted up on Timberlodge."

"I trust we stay in this camp tonight," Seabring said, his mind taking his thoughts in another direction. "I need my instrument to set up for celestial observations. It's been a too long time I have not, and there is considerable gap in my data log."

"I hope Ryerson appreciates the time we put in on his swimmin' hole," Cap went on, paying little attention to Seabring's work or his words. "I'll probably be stiff in the morning."

"Especially favorable is the viewing of Jupiter and Mars just now from this location on the planet and hemisphere."

"But then if we ride for Fort Walker in the morning, bouncing around all day in the saddle ought to loosen up any stiffness and cramps I wake up with." Cap's words had a cynical tone.

"You might care in the desert to join me for my

observations tonight, Cap. In this clear air my little instrument defines some of the planetary surface features with remarkable resolution and clarity."

"Once, I guess back when I was in my fifties, I thought maybe gold prospecting would be safer and easier than continuing to chance getting popped out of the saddle by an outlaw .44. Turned out swinging a pick and shovel and standing ass-deep in a mountain stream with a gold pan wasn't my cup of tea neither. Had the ague or the miner's epizootic most of the time. Bones and muscles ached with rheumatiz and lumbago. I stood it three months and went home and pinned my badge back on. Besides them pick and shovel handles blessed me with a handful of horn calluses that cramped my gun-handling style and speed and that bothered me. First week back I laid low an *hombre* with a thousand-dollar price on his head, dead or alive, and that made up for my prospecting grubstake twice over and was sure more than any gold I found!"

"I've also seen Saturn's rings remarkably well," Seabring said, busy fondling and polishing his beloved telescope.

"Yeah, Doc," Cap went on, rambling. "A man ought to stay at what he's cut out for and best at. Like now. Here I am, on Ryerson's posse takin' in the likes of Bad-Face Ike. If I was out prospectin', I'd've missed all this."

Seabring had finished burnishing and mounting his telescope for his night's observation "Do you suppose one of us should go out and relieve Spunky, Cap?"

"What's that you say, Doc? Spunky? I was just

thinking that maybe one of us ought to go out and relieve him."

"That's what I just said, Cap."

"That's what I thought, too. Suppose we'd ought to take him a cup of this warmed-over breakfast coffee? It's strong enough to take the scale off his teeth, but at least it's good and hot."

Dr. Seabring made a face.

"Maybe we could both sit out there and guard the car, Doc. We could continue the nice conversation we've been having. Sure have enjoyed talking with you." Cap gingerly toted a steaming tin cup of hot, leftover coffee as the pair followed a lately tramped trail along the rim of the slough under the cottonwoods toward the sidetrack and their makeshift boxcar jail.

Coming out of the bower of trees where the car should have been, Seabring and Donovan were greeted with a shock of alarm by an empty, desolate siding and a wind chanting mournfully through the chaparral and the cottonwood limbs.

"Doc, the boxcar! It's gone."

"By all empirical evidence," Seabring agreed, dryly, his eyes examining closely the area for clues where the boxcar had stood.

"But what happened?"

"I can this assure you, Cap; it did not go straight up. Neither did it go sidewise. That narrows the possibilities to east or west. I paid little heed at the time, but I recall surmising that from the east the sound approached. We were busy and talking and I didn't think much more about it. I recall feeling that briefly the train must have stopped."

"So where's Spunky?" Cap looked around him, pivoting his head and then his body. "He's not around here." He raised his voice. "Spunky! Hey! Spunkeeeee!" The only response was the dirgelike sigh of the light ground wind rustling the chaparral and the juniper and piñon.

"Something must've happened to him, Doc."

Seabring spoke matter-of-factly. "Easy, Cap. We heard no gunshots, and of a body there's no sign. My reasoning is that somehow he's an unwilling passenger on the train. Otherwise, he would have come to confer with us."

Donovan's voice grew shrill with anxiety. "Then he's in big trouble. All alone with Bodene's gang in that boxcar. At least he's probably got his Winchester and his sidearm."

"Captain Donovan," Seabring cautioned, "I am just as concerned as you and as fearful for Spunky's safety. The situation calls for a clear and level head. You're excited."

"Who's excited, for Pete's sake?" Cap blurted. "I'm not excited! What're we gonna do?" His voice was still shrill.

"There are in the train crew also decent, strong men, Cap. Spunky's not alone. It's a time for logic. Break camp in all haste, but in good order. Ride west to intercept Cole and the others. That train to the best of my recollection was here about eleven this morning. By learning if Cole was along the tracks and at what time and if he saw a train, I extrapolate train's speed and Ryerson's location when we meet him and determine if indeed Spunky's train went west."

Cap was confused but encouraged by Seabring's

scientific approach. "I follow your line of reasoning," he said.

"I'd hazard the speculation that no train passed Cole and the others and that Spunky's train returned east. Call it gut feeling, however educated. It delimits the direction of our search—east—but that in no way simplifies our dilemma. From there, our reducing agent will be to determine the next feasible town at which Spunky's train would in all likelihood stop."

Cap figured he'd heard enough scientific mumbo jumbo. "Then let's get about breaking camp and going to find Cole! What the hell should I do with this coffee?"

"If left to me, my dear Captain Donovan, I'd drink it!"

For forty minutes of his madcap excursion atop the boxcar, Spunky clutched his Winchester and the running board planking to keep himself low in the face of a hammering headwind sweeping from the onrushing engine and flinging grit that, despite his cowering, filled his eyes and ears, his mouth and hair, and invaded his clothing. The admixture of soot, grit, and fly ash impacted with the sympathetic flow of mucus in his nostrils, the concretion clogging them to impair his breathing as the howling wind sucked away his breath through nose or mouth. Fighting a panic that went with it, he gasped and wheezed, filled with a terror close to suffocation.

Beside him telegraph poles whizzed past in almost heartbeat cadence; for a time he was mesmerized watching their gleaming fine filament copper strands dip and rise, dip and rise unendingly, punctuated by the blinking passage of sun-glistening blue glass insulators on brown-weathered crossarms.

The hell-bent pace unrelieved, Spunky felt himself on the verge of madness in his anxiety and inability to come to grips with the quandary; something had to be done.

In his mind the die was cast; his only hope lay with the engine crew. He raised up in a crouch, clutching the Winchester. He could not afford—at any cost—to lose it.

He measured the distance from the protruding end of the boxcar's running boards across an abyss to the padlike top of the engine tender and coal car ahead of him; the flat rear steel plate, he knew, covered a giant water reservoir for the engine's boiler and made up at least a third of the tender. Ahead of it, he also knew, was the giant hopper of handy coal for the hot, hungry maw of the locomotive's firebox.

Spunky rose up, bracing himself against being hurled off by the elemental headwind. He judged his jump at fewer than five feet. But he'd need a running start. He backed a respectable distance along the roof planking, grasping his Winchester. "Ready, set, go!" he yelled, and leaped to race ten long striding steps that against the wind were like running uphill in sand and vaulted across the impossible chasm.

The balls of his feet curled downward to contact the rim of the tender's rear steel plate, and for a split second he nearly pitched back into the yawning crevice over the couplers. Waving his rifle-impeded arms for balance, yet somehow impelled by forward momentum, he was boosted ahead and in a frantically hopped skipping motion, established himself on the top of the water tank. Taking no time to ponder the near failure of his feat, he swiftly strode to the high rim of the coal pile, looking down the ebony slope into the squared-off open locomotive cab. Both the engineer, perched on a square black upholstered seat at the right, peering ahead out the window past the engine's enormous black boiler, and the fireman, leaning out a similar opening to his left, were unaware of anyone else for miles. Both wore railroader's striped overalls.

Still leaning into the onrushing torrent of wind, Spunky—to accentuate his peaceful intent—levered open the Winchester, palmed the captured live round in the left hand that held the ineffectual rifle aloft, and shouted, "Hey!"

Again his words lost themselves downwind. Realizing they couldn't hear over the engine's roar, he picked up a fist-sized clod of gritty coal and under-handed it to thud and bounce on the steel plate of the cab floor.

Both engineer and fireman, their astonished, sweated faces begrimed with soot and fly ash, turned toward him, expressions fearful, their hands raised; the locomotive, its throttle tied, continued to plummet eastward. He wasn't totally certain the engineer might not have a long-barreled Colt along with the wrenches and long-spouted oil can nearby his perch at the cab's side window; he suddenly regretted unloading the Winchester.

His arms and open rifle raised, Spunky aped a broad grin.

"It's okay," he called lightly, certain they couldn't hear him, accentuating his lips' forming of the words. "I'm a friend."

The two in the cab apparently—because of their noisy trade—were fair lip-readers; they softened their tense posture and expressions. The engineer waved Spunky a brusque welcome.

He began a pell-mell stride down the coal chute, nearly falling in the slippery avalanche, finally setting his brakes a few inches shy of the firebox door.

"What you doin' here, mister?" the engineer demanded gruffly.

"Now don't get your underwear gnarled," Spunky called over the roar of the cab. "I was on top of that boxcar when you hooked on to it back down the line."

"That's contrary to Southern and Central procedure," the engineer insisted. "The directors don't allow no unauthorized passengers. Al said so."

The engineer was ruddy-faced with alert, sparkling eyes and fat cheeks going to jowls. The hair under his soft-billed striped railroad cap was steel gray.

Spunky glanced at the fireman; it was the man who had thrown the switches and coupled the boxcar to the engine tender. He was younger and leaner than the engineer, his face more open and friendly.

"I ain't of unlawful intent," Spunky insisted. "I'm a duly sworn deputy U.S. marshal from back down the line where you fellas hooked on to that car yonder."

"What was you doing unauthorized on a Southern and Central car?"

"I was on top standing guard. We got a dozen and a half outlaw prisoners locked up in there."

"You what?!"

"Sure as I'm a foot tall."

"That's also unauthorized use of railroad rolling stock," the engineer growled. "Al's really gonna bawl *me* out now. If you're a lawman, let me see your badge."

Spunky turned testy; after his ordeal, his patience was only a veneer. "I don't have to show you no stinking badge!" The words exploded out of him. "I'm duly sworn to duty under Marshal Cole Ryerson out of Fort Walker. We were taking in Bad-Face Ike Bodene's gang mostly for robbing this here very same railroad. We were doing just fine till you came along."

The engineer looked past Spunky at the fireman. "Wait till Al hears about this!"

"What's that about?" Spunky demanded.

"Al ought to give you and old King Cole a medal for catching Bad-Face Ike, but he ain't going to. The railroad company blamed him for the robbery for not looking after things better, and Al got royally bawled out. When Al gets bawled out by the brass collars, it's sure everybody up and down the line is going to catch hell from him. Al's never been one to take it alone, especially after the bosses called him on the carpet, which they do fairly frequent."

"Who's Al?" Spunky asked, his voice still impatient.

"Why, mister, he's Al Bumpshas, the Southern and Central general agent, yardmaster and master mechanic in Deep Purple Falls, next town down the line. Snottiest little prick the Sewer and Cesspool ever put on the payroll. We'll be there in exactly thirty minutes."

"Oh no, we won't," Spunky declared. "'Cause

you're stopping right here and running that car back to that siding where you found it. I stand by the authority of Marshal Cole Ryerson and the United States government!"

"Oh, no we ain't, Mr. Lawman. The eastbound Number Seven's less than five minutes behind us right now with a bunch of freight and passengers. I been ballin' the jack ever since pickin' up that deadhead at Coyote Siding to make sure I don't have Number Seven's headlight beamin' straight up my ass."

"I guess you got me there," Spunky confessed, turning meek again.

"Was I you, Mr. Lawman, I'd slick down my hair and dust off my boots and get ready to face the wrath of Mr. Alvin Bumpshas." A sardonic grin cut the engineer's face. When he spoke again, his intonation was nasal, like the loud projection of a passenger train conductor: "Twenty-five minutes to Deep Purple Falls. Next stop, Deep Purple Falls!"

Spunky looked out the window past the engineer's head with dismay and despair at the chaparral whizzing past in a blur.

"Why me?" he moaned again to himself. "Why does everything always happen to *me?*"

14

The Deep Purple Falls train yards were a bewildering welter of rails and switches on both sides stretching away in front of them as well as behind, some of the long sections of track choked with strings of boxcars. Frank and Hank, the engineer and fireman respectively, switched and shunted their engine and single car into a vacant sidetrack between rows of boxcars, which shut off the view on all sides. Frank explained:

"Now you just watch and see that main line we come in on, Mr. Spunky Deputy Marshal. We cleared ahead of Number Seven by no more'n a hop-skip-jump. Depot's up east a mile yet, so he'll be pouring the coal to her highballin' past here. Main line's right there next to Hank's elbow. You could go stand on the plate there above the steps behind Hank and get ready for the thrill of your life. Don't stick your head out too far. Old Number Seven'll kick up a draft that'll suck you off the platform or at least whack your old bean

165

against the side of the cab yonder. Men been known to lose their marbles that way."

Though Spunky hadn't gotten much more from the trainmen by way of information to brace him for his encounter with Al Bumpshas, they had introduced themselves by first name only, and Spunky had responded with his.

What Frank had described as the main line was just another set of tracks beside their sidetracked engine and the boxcar full of Bad-Face Ike's gang. Across the main line from them, a seemingly endless queue of silent boxcars blocked the sky and stretched away in both directions; again Spunky felt closed in and suffocated. He looked at the almost touchable travelworn freight car on the siding across the main line from where he stood at the rear and one side of the engine cab. Convenient vertical grab irons were close to him at the end of the coal tender and at the side of the engine cab. Spunky clutched one in each hand for support and leaned out between the cab and tender to look back west along the lonesome, empty track. Out there, as though down a long tunnel of sidelined freight cars, he could see a ribbon of sky over him and a small, narrow patch of daylight where the strings of railroad cars ended. Spunky sensed panic born of confinement. Suddenly he yearned for the random openness of the magnificent trees of Timberlodge.

Down that narrow chasm framed by tall wheeled boxes, his ears perked to a distant, piercing "whoo-who-whoo" of the oncoming train's whistle. A black plug with a sharp yellow light in its center blocked the space and crowded out the sky on all sides; in the close quarters, the roaring sound charging ahead of it terrified Spunky but fired his blood with excitement.

With a thunderous clickety-clack, Number Seven roared down the narrow chute to petrify Spunky and rob him of his breath as it plummeted past with an enormous swirl and suck of heat, noise, and dust. The black locomotive rocketed by, with the swaying, rocking baggage and express cars and several freight cars but bats of an eye in time announcing the immediate rhythmic and uncountable white-lighted windows of two day coaches.

As suddenly as it appeared, Number Seven was gone, its muted clacking cadence receding up the track. Spunky poked his head out farther to watch the rear vestibule disappear in the distance. He made out the forms of a man in the crisp Navy blue and brass outfit and properly fitted stiff visored cap of a train conductor smoking a cigarette, and a woman in a flowing, swirling burgundy gown, matching large hat and parasol doing the same on the last car's rear platform. The train's whistle hooted a code of longs and shorts again, and Spunky distinguished the sounds of the squeals and lurches of the train braking for its stop beside the Deep Purple Falls passenger depot platform.

Frank and Hank gathered up their belongings, blue denim jackets, and wicker lunch hampers and moved to get down from the engine cab.

"All out for the Deep Purple Falls Southern and Central train yards, Mr. Deputy Marshal," Frank announced breezily. "Night crew's gonna make up a train of empties with that one back yonder. Number

Five's goin' outta here tomorra morning' at six with her string of deadheads for the Frisco docks. Guess you got till then to figure what to do with your prisoners back yonder. Maybe Al Bumpshas'll help ya. But I wouldn't count on it. Al more'n likely'll throw *you*—and them—in the calaboose!"

Spunky's heart sank as he dropped down to the uneven slag boulders of the roadbed, his feet and legs now unaccustomed to solid footing; they wanted to continue walking on a swaying surface, and he staggered like a man with too much of a cargo of Cole Ryerson's Old Group Tightener.

"Come on, Spunky," Frank trumpeted. "Hank and me'll show you the yard office and point out Al Bumpshas to ya. Hank and me are off work soon's we punch out. You get finished up with Al in time, you come on over to the Sewer and Cesspool—beggin' your pardon, Southern and Central—Rai'road Hotel, roomin' house, beanery, saloon, pool hall, and sometimes a whorehouse—back there next to the tracks yonder, we come right by it—and let Hank and me buy you a tank of beer for old times' sake. We'll be there a couple of hours. Right, Hank? You get through with Al, you're gonna need one, Spunky. And deserve it. Maybe two. Come on, Lawman!"

Spunky followed as the trainmen in grimy denim led him a merry chase in a maze of rails, boxcars, flatcars, and gondolas, zigzagging to leapfrog over convenient couplers; Spunky wondered how in hell he'd ever find the boxcar and Bad-Face Ike Bodene's gang again. He figured by now Ryerson was having a stroke.

At last his two companions leaped over the last coupler into a vast open graveled area crowded by imposing shop buildings mostly of brick and stone. Roadways and here and there a line of open rails crisscrossed the yard, some leading into the shops themselves. Tradesmen in greasy denims similar to those of Hank and Frank seemed to mill around, carrying tools, materials, or lumber; everywhere Spunky looked was hustle and bustle.

"Welcome to the Deep Purple Falls yards of the Sewer and Cesspool Rai'road, Spunky," Frank declared. "Everything's here, roundhouse, boiler shop, blacksmith shop, wood mill, repair tracks large and small, everything to fix and maintain a rai'road and rollin' stock. And just about everything's run from that place yonder, the little house. We call it the yard office."

The place Frank gestured at indeed looked like a small house with no frills or flowers. It had some sort of composition roofing, its siding freshly painted an uninspiring blue-gray.

"You'll find the jasper who pulls all the strings around here in there. You just go in and ask to see Mr. Bumpshas. I wouldn't suggest you start off calling him Al."

"Couldn't you fellas stick around just a bit?" Spunky asked meekly. "Kind of to back up my story of how I come to be here?" He was at the point of needing all the moral support he could get.

"Frank and me got to punch out over at the paymaster's shanty," Hank, the fireman, confessed.

"Yeah," Frank said. "You go on ahead and get

things straightened out with Al Bumpshas, and if you got time before you leave town, come on down and have a beer with us. The s'loon's yonder under the roomin' house. They call it the Southern and Central Hotel."

With that and without another word of hope or encouragement, Hank and Frank disappeared around the corner of the nearby yard office, leaving Spunky feeling abandoned to the wolves, but realizing as well that the two trainmen had no stake in his dilemma. He squared his shoulders. The only way to get it done and get Bad-Face Ike's gang back to Cole Ryerson was to screw up his courage and confront the terrible-tempered Al Bumpshas. The door to the squat gray building had a small window at the top, but the sun's reflection wouldn't let him see in. He wondered if he'd oughtn't to knock but decided against it.

Inside, several clerks toiled at desks in a good-sized bay area of closely packed desks with what appeared to be several closed-door offices along one side and the back wall. The place smelled pungently of grease, pencil shavings, and tobacco smoke.

A youngish clerk wearing a green eyeshade with a yellow pencil pried on top of his ear looked up. He wore a slender black tie and white shirt with sleeve bands to hold his shirt cuffs above his wrists. His shirtsleeves, however, were hidden under blousy dark cloth wristlets almost to his elbows.

"You lookin' for somebody?" the clerk asked.

"Here to see Mr. Bumpshas," Spunky said with as much authority as he could muster.

The clerk studied Spunky's disheveled and dingy

range clothing and the disreputable-looking character wearing them.

"Are you expected?"

"Well, ah, as a matter of fact, no."

"He's pretty busy."

The small talk took the edge off Spunky's timidity and his eyes narrowed, his forbearance wearing thin.

"I'm a deputy United States marshal. You tell him that."

"I'm just a clerk. You'll have to tell him yourself. See that aisleway between the desks and that door at the end? That's Mr. Bumpshas's office. He's busy, and Mr. Bumpshas, he don't like to be disturbed when he's busy, which is most of the time."

"Well," Spunky growled, his fuse close to setting off the main charge, "I got business with him that won't keep."

He walked through a waist-high swinging door in a low wall that separated the entrance from the clerks' work area. Spunky noted that the inside of the place was painted with the same monotone blue-gray as the yard office's exterior.

A dulled brass plate on the closed door had been crudely die-stamped with the words: A. E. Bumpshas, General Agent, Yardmaster. This time Spunky knocked.

The response was something between a bark and a growl. "Yeah?"

"Need to talk to you, Mr. Bumpshas."

"I'm busy."

"I'm a deputy marshal," Spunky called through the door's thick panels. "Need to talk to you."

"You servin' papers?" The voice now was a definite growl.

"Nawsir. My business is of another nature."

"All right. Come on in."

Spunky opened the door tentatively and stepped in. The man behind the desk resembled nothing more than an irate bulldog, and built much the same. A greasy and sweat-stained felt hat was perched on the back of his stump-sized head. His mouth and undershot jaw were clamped on a scant inch of cigar butt, which jutted like a fixture from his face. He wore the grimy vest and pants of a herringbone tweed suit. Spunky could see that the pants bagged at the knees as Bumpshas had his work-broganned feet propped on his desk while he pored over papers and reports. The misshapen baggy tweed coat hanging on a nearby hat tree also had plenty of slack at the elbows; Al Bumpshas, clearly, was not dressed to the nines. Not even to the eights.

The eyes in the bulldog head were piglike, tiny and blinking, the lids pink with prominent bleached lashes.

"You don't look like no marshal. Where's your hat? You look like a hobo to me. State your bidness. I'm busy."

"One of your engines brought in a carload of fugitives, and I gotta take 'em back."

Bumpsha's brogans dropped off the desk, and he spit out the soggy cigar stub to squash on the floor on impact. "What!?" Now his voice was a bark.

"We had eighteen outlaws locked in a boxcar on a siding a long ways west of here, I don't know how far, and a couple of your guys named Hank and Frank hooked on to it and brought it all the way here, and the gang's out there now somewhere in that car in your train yard."

"Coyote Siding. That's in direct violation of Southern and Central policy. You got any kind of a shipper?"

"A shipper?"

"Paperwork. A proper invoice or authorization."

"Naw, we just put 'em in there for a little while till we could get horses to take 'em to Fort Walker."

"On whose authority?" Bumpshas demanded, and in the face of his fiery wrath, Spunky began to wither.

"United States Marshal Cole Ryerson." His words came out sounding timid.

"That son of a bitch!" Bumpshas growled, low and surly like the vicious bulldog he now fully resembled to Spunky. "Boot Hill Cole, my Aunt Tillie's left tit! Why in hell the gummint didn't fire that nincompoop and put his decrepit old fart boss Winfield out to pasture where he belongs years ago is one of the Seven Wonders of the World!"

Spunky, remembering his place as a Ryerson Renegade, tried to draw himself up haughtily. "Sir, you speak of one of the finest lawmen of the West. Not to mention my very good friend. I'll remind you to keep a civil tongue in your head where Cole Ryerson is concerned."

Bumpshas leaned forward on his desk and scowled. "Balderdash! What's your name, deputy?"

"Smith. Sylvester Smith."

"Well, Sylvester Smith, for your information, it's

common knowledge all over the Southern and Central that when Ike Bodene broke jail after Ryerson incarcerated him for the second time, he hit the Southern and Central express car to the tune of ten thousand dollars for no better reason than to taunt your precious Dung Hill Cole into a showdown to the death."

Al Bumpshas stood up angrily to stalk his office floor. Spunky nearly gasped; Bumpshas was an extremely short man, scarcely a few inches over five feet. Then he remembered the wisecrack about dynamite coming in small packages; he also remembered Frank the engineer calling Bumpshas a "little prick."

"If they'd've killed one another, it'd've been no skin off me," Bumpshas growled. "For my money, the world'd've been better served if they'd've done just that! It's no mystery I lump Ryerson and Bodene in the same peck basket when it comes to makin' my life a hell on earth!"

Bumpshas indignantly prowled a circle around the perimeter of his small office; Spunky found himself pivoting in place watching fascinated as the Southern and Central's pint-sized strong man in Deep Purple Falls paced the floor. By now Bumpshas seemed to talk to himself.

"Ryerson come down here after the train robbery, askin' a bunch of dumb questions, him and that Cactus Manure or whatever his name is."

"Maguire," Spunky corrected with a spurt of indignation. "Cactus Jack Maguire. He's dead. One of Bodene's men done it."

"No great loss to the world," Bumpshas commented callously without batting an eye. "Wasn't much to him to begin with. Wandered around out there in the shops, eyes big as soup bowls and sunburnin' the roof of his mouth, taking it all in like he'd never been more five miles outta Fort Walker, which there ain't a hell of a lot up there to recommend that place neither."

Spunky bristled and was on the verge of popping him one. There wasn't much to Bumpshas, either, and what there was, Spunky decided, was mostly mouth. But he'd always been told only to pick on somebody his own size. In this case, he'd have his hands full if he tried to cut this shrimp down to a smaller size.

"They went away," Bumpshas went on, "this Dung Hill Cole and Cactus Manure, and nothing ever came of it except I come damn close to losin' my meal ticket over that robbery with the head office in K.C.—that's Kansas City, to you." For the first time in several sentences, Bumpshas acknowledged Spunky. "I got called on the carpet. Had to go clear back there to answer to a special meeting of the gawdam S and C tribunal, if you can imagine getting bawled out by seven feeble, fine-haired old fossils in succession and then in unison. Hell, I bet I sweat off twenty pounds that afternoon. The express company dropped their contract and took that ten thousand out of their hides in court, and the old bastards damn near got mine in part payment." Bumpshas still spoke from deep bitterness.

He spun around angrily to face Spunky, hitting him with a glare that put a blistering sun to shame. "As if that wasn't enough, here you are, Smith, with your cock-and-bull story that Ryerson took it upon himself to stow Bad-Face Ike's gang in one of my boxcars without authorization. On top of that, they got a free ride to Deep Purple Falls."

"But . . ." Spunky started.

"No ifs, ands, or buts!" Bumpshas yelled, and Spunky shrunk again. The last time he'd heard that phrase, Ryerson was ordering him back to Fort Walker to give Bertha Maguire the dread news about Cactus Jack. He remembered the agony of that trip.

Bumpshas's jaw was still unhinged and flapping. "I got no tender feelings for Dung Hill Cole and his unauthorized use of my railroad. And since that's the case, I'll calculate the freight charges, figure a special charter fee, and since you're a nice fella, Smith, I'll knock off a discount for haulin' passengers in a freight car. I figure it ought to come out to about a hundred dollars, cash money. On the barrelhead."

Spunky blanched. "You ain't expecting me to . . ."

A wicked gleam darted from Bumpshas's eyes, and Spunky finally got it that the crook schemed to pocket the money himself. "You're Ryerson's authorized representative, ain't you?! You come in here yellin' about that loud enough! You damn betcha I expect you to. You got the money to pay the fee?"

"No."

"How much you got?"

"Seventeen dollars and thirty-two cents!"

Another evil smirk now crossed Al Bumpshas's features. "Well, then we'll just get the town constable to lock you up—you and Bad-Face Ike and his boys—in his bullpen over to the city jail till Dung Hill Cole shows up to stand good for his fees to the Southern and Central. And Mulrooney's going to need

176

his costs took care of for the feed of that gang and the charges for keepin' you and Bodene in the lockup all that time."

"That constable'll never do that!"

Bumpshas laughed out loud. "Constable Mulrooney about doubles his town wages servin' as railroad dick for the Southern and Central on the side. So just don't assume too much cooperation in your behalf on the part of a fellow lawman."

Spunky was speechless.

"I'll work up a proper invoice, and soon as you sign the statement of charges, you and I'll go over in the train yard and check on the condition of your dunnage."

"Dunnage?"

"Your cargo, for want of a better word. Them outlaws."

"But I can't sign and authorize for a hundred dollars!"

"Well, then, sir, that freight car is going to be made up into a train of deadheads—empties—bound for the Frisco docks in the mornin'. I'll have my train crew haul them boys three or four hundred miles out into no-man's-land and turn 'em loose. Then we'll all be shed of Mr. Bad-Face Ike, and my friend Dung Hill Cole'll wind up with the egg on his face for a change."

Spunky gritted his teeth while an old refrain rang in his head. *Why me? Why does everything happen to me?*

"I'll sign your paper, Mr. Bumpshas," he said reluctantly.

"I figured you'd come to your senses. Cash money," Bumpshas said.

"Cole'll probably be good for it. But he doesn't even know where I am. Probably thinks I'm dead."

"Don't start with the sad music, deputy. Ryerson knows that anything that happens on this railroad we wind up knowin' about sooner or later. He'll come nosin' in here one of these days askin' around."

Spunky rolled his eyes, totally perplexed.

15

Ten minutes later, Al Bumpshas folded up and stuffed in the inside breast pocket of his stained, baggy tweed suit coat an official-looking form charging Ryerson a hundred dollars for services rendered and signed by Sylvester Smith as proxy.

Almost running to keep up with the rapid churning of Al Bumpshas's stubby legs, and again hopping over couplers and struggling along rough slag roadbeds between rows of boxcars, Spunky made his troubled way back to the car and the source of all his misery, Bad-Face Ike. Bumpshas strode up to the car door, its heavy hasp still secured to the eye by a stout stick; he beat on the door with the side of his fist.

"Bodene! You in there?" He got no response and turned to look quizzically at Spunky. He pounded again. "Hey, Ike!"

He turned to Spunky. "You sure this is the car?"

"This is the one. Engine's still hooked on."

"We'll take a careful look-see. Maybe they all died in there from suffocation. Now that'd do my heart a great deal of good."

Spunky's own heart melted.

Bumpshas unhooked the hasp and reefed on the heavy door to carefully slide it open a few inches. "This is like lifting the lid on Pandora's box," he muttered out the side of his mouth to Spunky. "Want to make sure those bastards don't come boiling out of there into my lap." He stuck his face close to the crack, looking into the car before belting out a hearty guffaw; he flung the door open all the way to stop with a rattling thud at the end of its track.

"Your troubles are over, Smith. Ryerson's outlaws flew the coop!" Spunky heard distinct gloating in his voice.

Spunky crowded close to see for himself. The boxcar was empty as a stepmother's heart. On the opposite wall, bringing a spear of shock to Spunky's frame, a duplicate door stood wide open.

Bumpshas continued to laugh, almost hysterically. He pulled Spunky's signed invoice from his pocket and gleefully tore it to bits and threw it into the air like confetti.

"The great Dung Hill Cole!" Bumpshas howled in merriment. "Locked this side up tight as a bull's ass in fly time and forgot the door on the other side! Bad-Face Ike is back on the loose somewhere between here and Coyote Siding! You're cleared of all responsibility, Smith! I got no evidence at all that you ever hauled any men to town in that car. You go tell Dung Hill Ryerson the laugh's on him and what a big heart Al Bumpshas has got, 'cause he ain't charging you for your hundred-or-so-mile ride. So, you go back and tell the clever Mr. Marshal Ryerson about this one!"

Bumpshas spun his stubby frame on one heel and strode off down the tracks and climbed between the couplers and disappeared.

Spunky stood, totally confused, as a heavy silence and a deep depression descended over him like a gray cloud.

Hazing their small horse herd back toward the Southern and Central right-of-way from Camp Walker, Bertha Maguire rode carefree as a skylarking schoolgirl. Ryerson observed that she sat her horse like a champion. They were not half an hour on the trail out of Camp Walker, he mused, before she had the motley, buzzard-bait band of army packhorse rejects and old out-to-pasture campaigners practically eating out of her hand as though they'd known her all their lives.

Again Ryerson was glad she was along, delighted to hear the cheerful chirp of her voice raised sweetly but firmly in urging the horses along. She had a fine sharp whistle as well that perked the ears of any thinking of quitting the bunch.

Cole found himself uncommonly pleased with everything, almost euphoric. Aside from the loss of Cactus Jack, they had corralled Bad-Face Ike virtually without incident. He was sure that Hans, Cap, and Spunky would have a fine camp waiting for them when they got in. He figured that with any kind of luck, they'd be back home in Fort Walker in fewer than two days.

Well before Ryerson, Bertha, and Fernando reached

the twin iron strands of the Southern and Central, the horses had settled into the trail routine.

Ryerson laid a great deal of it to their care and upbringing as army horses. Fernando was no slouch when it came to horse savvy, but Bertha, Ryerson observed, possessed that elusive magic touch and encouraging words that kept them willing and obedient and demonstrating a coltlike enthusiasm he hadn't expected of broken-down army nags.

Riding out of Camp Walker after an irritating and frustrating negotiation about the horses with the icy, uppity, and imperious camp commandant, Major Frederick "Frozen" Locke, Ryerson apologized to Fernando as he asked him to ride drag.

"We're gonna have our hands full, *amigo,*" he explained with Fernando's faithful eyes following and burning into his for instructions. "I'll ask you to watch things back here. But you may have to come up the sides now and then to keep 'em bunched. I'll ride back once in a while and spell you."

"It's no *problema,* Meester Ryerson. Eighteen horses what you call easy . . . cup of tea."

"You mean duck soup."

"Same like it. You stay up at point yonder, with Meesuss Cactus Jack. I like it here." Fernando flashed a tooth-gleaming grin at Ryerson and swung his horse around to position himself at the rear of the remuda.

For a moment, Ryerson watched Fernando's back as he rode down the line to take up his rear guard position. Inwardly he swelled with pride; he'd picked well the members of his *posse comitatus.* With a flick of the reins and a heel nudge, he guided Jo Shelby around to rejoin Bertha at the head of the column.

He had wondered briefly how well the very thorough housewife and cook, Bertha Maguire, would do as a horse wrangler.

Ryerson's astonishment wasn't long in coming. As he watched slack-jawed, she responded to the horses and rode among them as she did with any person who didn't fully comprehend her. She let them know firmly and without the fretting of a fishwife exactly who was boss in the area under her control and that she'd brook no interference with her judgments.

The army horses, bred and accustomed to commands, quickly learned who was in the saddle. Ryerson himself quickly learned that after Bertha communicated her authority to the leaders firmly but pleasantly, the two of them could ride in traditional swing positions about a third of the way back in the herd on either side; the hard-packed gravel wagon road from Camp Walker to the rail line gave the lead horses all the bearings and coordinates they needed. The message was somehow transmitted back down the line and the remuda swung into line obediently, lowered their heads, and played follow the leader.

Traveling beside the column opposite Bertha, he glanced back to see Fernando riding easily but alert to one side of the stirred-up dust cloud. Ryerson allowed himself to relax and be lulled and massaged by Jo Shelby's plodding gait.

A break came in the column, and he swung Jo Shelby next to Bertha's horse as the dozen and a half slab-sided old army cayuses strung out through the chaparral jogged along, even acting a bit frisky at being on the move again and perhaps looking forward to seeing a little action.

"How do you do it, Bertha Maguire?" Ryerson called. "Where'd you learn your horse handling?"

"I thought you knew, Cole. Dad bred and raised horses as well as cattle back home in Texas. He thought the range country and cattle trail life was too rough for a girl, so I got a lot of experience with the horses on the ranch. I think he thought the cowboy life might make me a coarse person. His decision also kept me close to home to help my mother, who was the best cook and homemaker in West Texas."

"So that's how you got your start. And church every Sunday."

Bertha looked at him. "And church every Sunday."

"Permit me a compliment, Mrs. Maguire, but you are an extraordinary woman. I thought that before you signed on, and not much has happened to tarnish that impression."

Bertha's acknowledgment was handled in a quick look of appreciation. "My folks raised me to be gentle and ladylike but not soft, Cole."

"If I haven't apologized for my behavior when you showed up at Dave Nesler's cabin the other day, let me do that now. I had a lot on my hands along about then. A great deal of my discourtesy had nothing to do with your presence."

"Thank you, Cole," she said sweetly. "I wasn't myself either with my feelings over John's death."

Ryerson's eyes on hers held a philosophical depth. "We both were under a strain. John was one of the finest men I'd ever worked with. Despite our scrap when you showed up at Timberlodge, I couldn't help but admire your courage in the face of his death."

The army's wagon road reached the Southern and

Central right-of-way; without a word, Bertha and Cole moved closer to the lead horses to guide them in a column left maneuver to bend the line of plodding horseflesh and begin their eastward trek through the chaparral bordering the rail line.

"I won't lie to you, Cole," she continued after the horses had settled into the new direction. Now they rode close to the leaders, guiding them through trackless territory. "John's death bit and bit deeply. I worshipped him. Because of the nature of the work he loved, though, I told myself years ago that the day might come that a man like Spunky would knock on my door with just such a message as he delivered. Until that time came, I determined not to allow it to cloud my thoughts nor my relationships, especially with John. And I didn't. In other words, I was ready, and fortunately faith in God had a great deal to do with my responding with dignity and strength."

Ryerson squirmed in the saddle; he'd never felt that level of closeness with a Supreme Being but admired others who did. "I guess when Spunky was so long getting back, I realized you'd be with him." he explained. "I knew it would be out of character for you to cave in and go hide under the covers."

"John respected and admired you so much, Cole."

Ryerson felt a pang of emotion, but the talk was going deeper than he cared to probe. It was almost with relief—but mixed with alarm—that he saw a dust cloud a half mile ahead and two riders coming at a steady, determined canter.

"We'll have to hold our thoughts about John till later, Bertha. See there. Out ahead."

"I've been watching them," she said.

"I recognize Hans's straw hat and Cap's white hair. Spunky's not with 'em. They know better than to ride off with only one man guarding Bad-Face Ike. Something's dead wrong!"

While Spunky Smith tried to sort out his misfortunes over a schooner of beer with Hank and Frank—the only people he knew in Deep Purple Falls—Enrico Garibaldi, the Italian cook in the kitchen of the "dining room," more properly the rooming house beanery next to the saloon, saw red when his favorite butcher knife, a massive wide and razor-sharp blade, turned up missing, probably stolen by someone when his back was turned. He had an idea who'd taken it.

Furious in a white-hot Italian rage, Garibaldi charged out the kitchen's open back door into the broad sunlight of the alley to find his suspect, the orphaned little black street urchin named Joshua who loitered around in the alley living off scraps from Garibaldi's kitchen.

"Hey, you little-ah sheet!" Garibaldi yelled at the instantly cringing Joshua. "Why you-ah steal my goddammah bootchah knife-ah, hah?! Ain't-ah Garibaldi bin-ah good to you?"

"Ah din takes nuffin, Missuh Gahbally," Joshua pleaded. "But ah seen them two mans come out witcher knife an' run down da alley. Dey was black mans, but dey wun't no nigguhs like me."

At nearly the same moment, a wide-eyed, ashen-faced man in the grimy, greasy overalls of a Southern and Central shop worker, burst excitedly through the doors of the saloon where Spunky sat along the bar with Hank and Frank. Spunky quietly stared into the scumming suds in his nearly empty bucket of beer, his mind still in turmoil.

"Somebody killed Steve Mulrooney over to the constable's office!" the newcomer screamed to one and all in the saloon. "Damn near cut his neck clean off! Blood squirted clear to the ceiling and all over the wall. Hell of a mess! I just come by there after it happened. Looks like they stole all his guns and pistols and all his bullets!"

"Who done it?" somebody yelled.

"Damned if I know," the man said excitedly.

"I'm goin' down there and have a look-see," somebody else hollered.

That fast, the saloon's clientele, twenty or so customers, dulled by a quiet glass of beer at the end of a hard day's work, was energized. Drinks were gulped and cigarettes were snubbed out. At a backroom table, four poker players simply exposed their cards and high man took the pot. They jumped up to join the noisy exodus of others—Hank and Frank among them—thronging down the street to the late constable's office.

Fearing the worst, Spunky lingered at the bar, his emotional pangs stabbing even deeper now. A throat-cutting in Deep Purple Falls meant only one thing: Bad-Face Ike Bodene. The unlocked boxcar door must have jarred open, he decided, on the pell-mell race to Deep Purple Falls. When the word got out—and Al Bumpshas could be relied on to let the world know that Spunky Smith was responsible for bringing the outlaw curse to town—their committee for vigilance wouldn't hesitate before stringing Spunky up from the nearest telegraph pole as accessory to murder.

Feeling about as glum as any time he could remember, Spunky abruptly went rigid with alarm as the distant concussion of five well-spaced pistol shots shredded the saloon's dead silence; Spunky recoiled involuntarily on the bar stool with each of them.

"Oh, Lord," he moaned, burying his face in his hands. "Bad-Face Ike's really on a rampage."

Greater commotion outside brought him even further alert; he raced to the batwing doors to peer over them into the sunlit street. Shouts, the rolling tattoo of prancing hooves, and the bark of random pistol shots shattered the stillness that had crept back around Spunky after the first startling volley.

The fracas now sounded to him like a running gunfight.

From the direction the crowd had gone to view the chaos at the constable's office, a massed phalanx of a dozen horses, many with two riders, thundered up the street that ran between the town's grubby business section and the railroad tracks and past the saloon doors and the bewildered eyes of Spunky Smith. He wasn't bewildered long. The lead rider on a sleek gelding headed west wore the pock-marked mug of Ike Bodene. Spikelike Winchester barrels were as evident as bristles on a hog. Spunky, his heart shrinking inside him, knew all the rest of the riders by sight. Behind them came the hooting and shooting townsmen on foot.

Hurrying bootfalls of a man in the vanguard of the mob—most of them railroaders, from their outfits— thundering back from the constable's office, reached Spunky's ears as he stood rooted to his place behind the saloon's batwings.

"What the hell's goin' on?" Spunky yelled as the man jogged past on the board sidewalk chasing the retreating horses. "It's them," the runner replied, stopping momentarily, gasping for breath. "The outlaw bunch that's treed the town. Cut Steve Mulrooney's throat, stole all his guns. Bled to death. Poor son of a bitch. Then they pumped five shots into Lucius Cate at the livery stable. Killt him dead on the spot and run off with ever' hoss in the place. Now they're makin' their getaway west. Hear it's the same bunch that knocked over the S and C express car and took a lot of money a month or so back!"

"Bad-Face Ike," Spunky responded wistfully.

"The very jasper, right enough," the man replied, getting his wind back. "Well, I ain't gonna catch up with 'em. Might's well come in and have a beer."

Spunky stepped aside to let him enter.

Others, wearying of the chase after running up the street to the constable's and then back again, called it quits at the saloon doors and mobbed the place, buying beer and stouter stuff, euphoric with excitement, all talking at once about what they had seen and when and who said what to who, and how the victims looked, and how well they were acquainted with them in life.

Their yammering jangled Spunky's already frayed nerves; he sought a quiet corner of the saloon with a fresh beer to try to deal with these new and terrifying developments.

Bad-Face Ike had a long ride ahead of him, but there was no question in Spunky's mind but that Ike was on a collision course with Ryerson's Renegades now. Ryerson needed to be warned, but Spunky could figure no way of getting a message to him before the gang got to Coyote Siding or wherever Bodene found Ryerson's Renegades. He had no notion of the Southern and Central's timetable, or if they'd even let him off at an unscheduled stop. Spunky continued to futilely chase his mental tail as he dejectedly contemplated the beer foam drying in descending bathtub rings down the inside of his glass schooner.

"Well, well, Deputy Smith," a familiar voice intruded beside him. "The man responsible for all this killing and looting!"

An alarmed Spunky quickly looked around at who might have heard and then he looked up—but not that far—at the bulldog features of the runty Al Bumpshas. Spunky stayed silent, knowing there was more to come.

"Figured you'd be long gone, deputy." Bumpshas now wore his townsman's felt hat square on his head, the grimy tweed suit hanging in pouches from his stubby frame. The cremated, emasculated inch-long unlit remains of a black cigar was wedged at the corner of his mouth, gray with ash at one end and spittle-soggy at the other; Al Bumpshas was a man who chewed and smoked his tobacco at the same time.

"Guess I brought Ike Bodene here to raise all this particular hell," Spunky said with remorse and apology.

"I haven't told anybody about that," Bumpshas confessed.

"I appreciate it," he said, thinking Bumpshas had done a right proper job of it just moments before.

"Was I you, Smith, I'd get myself out of town without delay. Steve Mulrooney and Lucius Cate were respected men in this town. Feelings are running high about their murders. In your behalf, I've told Hank and Frank to keep mum, too."

Spunky regarded Bumpshas with a sort of awe; he hadn't expected such consideration after their earlier bitter encounter. "I need a horse," he told Bumpshas.

"Probably ain't one to be had after Bad-Face Ike ransacked the livery," Bumpshas said, and Spunky saw the hint of smirk. "And seventeen dollars and forty-eight cents won't buy you much."

"Seventeen dollars and thirty-two cents," he corrected.

"You're still suckin' hind tit, deputy."

"Cole Ryerson needs to be warned of a sneak attack by Ike Bodene, Mr. Bumpshas, whether you hold him in high regard or not. It just ain't a civil thing to do."

Bumpshas was unmoved. "Ryerson's on his own, just like you are. I'm still on thin ice with those fine-haired fossils in K.C. I had to wire them of the dire situation here with two townsmen dead and a mad dog on the loose and headed out our westbound right-of-way. They wired right back embargoing that train of deadheads due out of here that way first thing in the morning. It's postponed indefinitely. That's a fine kettle of fish! I got orders to fill, trains to make up. This kind of delay knocks things around here right into a cocked hat. Them Kansas City cretins don't take that into account. On top of that, them Nervous Nellies are worried about the eastbounds, too. A bunch like old Ike's could raise particular hell with a moving train. All it takes'd be a tie across the tracks or a couple of big rocks, and I got a wreck on my hands. So I'm still in hot water, Smith. Those old fogey pantywaists figure they hold me accountable for every owlhoot in the west and for every incompetent cop like Ryerson!"

"Well, then, what the hell am *I* supposed to do? I need a horse. Only way I'll get one is to steal it!"

"You get caught stealin' a horse around here, you're hanged pronto without benefit of law. Or clergy."

"No trains. No horses for sale. No money to buy one if there was. No friends, not any that gives a damn. If the town finds out who I am, I'm strung up right now. Hell of a mess."

"Was I you, Smith, I'd start out hoofing along the tracks west. You got a couple hours till dark."

"Hell, I got no grub. Ain't even got a blanket."

"Come on down to the office. I got an old blanket off a dead Injun I'll lend ya. Found him out in the train yard the other day, colder'n a mackerel."

Spunky was incredulous. "Lend me!?"

16

No westbounds came by, at least not since we've been in sight of the tracks," Ryerson explained to Donovan and Seabring as the trio pushed eastward for a trace of Spunky and the outlaws.

Bertha had gone to ride with Fernando and control the extra horses while the other three, riding in a point position ahead of the horse herd, held a council of war in the saddle.

"It's reasonable then, Cole, that a locomotive came from the east and hauled the car back that way," Seabring theorized.

"What were you fellas doing all that time?" Ryerson asked, the hint of an edge in his voice.

"Why up at the head end of that slough choppin' out that bathtub like you asked," Donovan said curtly. He didn't like Ryerson's tone that somehow he and Doc Seabring had let it all just happen.

Their patience already set on hair trigger, Ryerson

picked up Doc's attitude in his words as well. He felt himself going rigid; but for once, instead of shooting a response from the hip, he paused, grit his teeth, and spent a long moment looking into the distance. "Take it easy, Cap," he said. "We all got a lot on our minds. If I sound out of sorts, it ain't got to do with you. I'm gettin' tired of Ike Bodene giving me the slip every time my back's turned."

Donovan's tone also turned more conciliatory. "So we operate on the theory that Spunky and the boxcar went east. What's that way, Cole?"

"Seventy-five or eighty miles of nothing. Then a little place called Deep Purple Falls, headquarters and switch yards for the Central Division of the Southern and Central. Ain't none of it worth writin' home about."

Seabring's level scientist's voice intruded. "I suppose we have no course than to ride to Deep Purple Falls?"

Even with Seabring's calm words, Ryerson still sounded testy. "You got any better ideas, Hans? If they came and took away our boxcar, there'd be no reason for 'em to stop between here and there. We might find some clues or sign along the way, but I'm bettin' we won't know much till we get clear in there."

"Cap and I figured Spunky went against his will, or he would've come to tell us."

"Stands to reason, Hans," Ryerson said. "But why? How?"

"Ike's gang couldn't've gotten out and done anything," Cap put in. "They were unarmed and Spunky had his rifle and sidearm. Doc and I figured we'd've heard shooting."

"Could've happened lots of different ways," Ryerson said. "Maybe I should've insisted that two of you stay on guard all the time."

"Cat's out of the bag, Cole. It's done."

"Yeah, and I don't relish mounting a drive all the way to Deep Purple Falls playing mother hen to a spavined bunch of broke-down army cayuses neither. Locke made me sign a paper that I'd bring eighteen horses back. That ain't my worst pain in the neck, but it's sure one of a passel of 'em."

"Maybe you could ride there, Cole, and ask around," Cap suggested. "Leave us and the horses in camp at the slough."

Ryerson fixed another impatient squint on Donovan. "We'll not split the force again, Cap. I may err on the side of caution, but we're gonna plan our moves on the basis that Bad-Face Ike is abroad in the land again. I won't ride all the way there and back and risk returning empty-handed to a camp looted of horses and all my friends scattered around on the ground dead and scalped. Plus, if Ike catches me, the rest of you might as well pack up and go home. The party's over."

"We have all his guns, Cole," Seabring put in.

"And he could have a cache of arms somewhere, Hans. Naw, we push on to the slough, camp there tonight, post a strong guard, and head east in the morning. All of us. And the horses. We'll still need 'em when we catch up with Ike again."

"Then let's go back there and team up with Bertha and Fernando and get that remuda moving!" Cap said.

In the long moments of gray twilight before deep

dark descended on their orderly camp at the slough, Hans Seabring had spied a tall, flat-topped butte formation back toward the Timberlodge foothills. The outcropping was more a mesa, with a long sloping side a horse could negotiate to the top. He still itched to unlimber his telescope for his long-postponed nighttime probing of the heavens.

Cole Ryerson, he knew, was justifiably but overly edgy about the dangers. In his considered and scientific calculations of their situation with Ike Bodene, the empirical evidence at hand suggested that by the sheerest accident, the boxcar, with Spunky clinging aboard, was taken to this town of Deep Purple Falls.

His orderly equation further presumed that Spunky had contacted the authorities and dealt efficiently and effectively with the carload of outlaws. Perhaps even now, Spunky—with the outlaws safely under guard in a town jail—was again westbound by horse or by train to regain contact with Ryerson's Renegades.

His alternate theory, based on the worst that possibly could happen, persuaded him that if Bad-Face Ike was on the loose seventy-five or eighty miles away, finding horses and supplies for the trip back would be nearly impossible and would hold him up for days.

On that basis, he persuaded Ryerson to release him for a night of recording the goings-on in the star-choked realm overhead. The soft glow of a distant gibbous moon, misshapen as a lump of old yellow soap, lit Earth dimly without robbing the planets and stars of their glory—thus favoring Seabring's viewing, and the nearby mesa offered a superb vantage point.

"Hans," Ryerson cautioned, "you might be shavin'

it a bit thin, but all right," he continued, grinning, "go ahead. But do me one favor. I know you can set your all-knowing eye on free traverse. From up on that benchland, you ought to have clear view quite a long ways east. Practically almost to Deep Purple Falls. Give the country that way a sweep or two. If Ike's boys are runnin' wild again—and I have a hunch they are—and are in the vicinity, I'm bettin' they'll have a fire. The train line's straight as a die, and Ike'll not be far from it if he's headed back to find me around here. Just use your scope to have a look-see at the neighborhood and make sure the coast is clear. If he's got all his gang about him, they'll have a big night fire. If you spot anything amiss out there in the dark, you come a-runnin'!"

Bertha Maguire materialized into the wan light of their small campfire under the cottonwoods. "Would you have need of a helper, Dr. Seabring?" she asked eagerly. "Cole's told me of the wonders of the heavens that you bring close with your telescope."

Seabring looked across the fire at Cap Donovan, remembering he offered Cap such a chance the day before. A shadowy figure crouched almost beyond the fire's light, Donovan honed and stropped his sheath knife, oblivious to the talk.

"Cole?" Seabring began. "What do you think? All right for Mrs. Maguire to tag along?"

"I guess you won't be that far. That way, if we're ambushed, I'll fortunately have about half my force in reserve to hit their blind side. Take your Winchesters. And remember to harass the foe from the rear if we're attacked down here."

Three quarters of an hour later, Seabring had his

telescope deployed and elevated on his tripod for easy viewing from a comfortable standing position. Under the balmy night sky and its vivid canopy of stars and planets, Bertha watched the scientist at work with rapt attention, helping when she could.

Seabring shoved back his straw hat and dropped his pince-nez on their black-ribboned cord. Squinting one eye, he glued the other to the eyepiece. Two knob-activated ratchet devices allowed him to elevate the tube by degrees and laterally traverse the field of view in the same gradual way.

"Dark out there," he murmured to Bertha, possessed by his field of view through his eyepiece. "On the land, that is. Cole asked me to survey the area east of our position for any signs of activity. There's barely enough light to see the rail lines; haven't found 'em yet . . . Aha! There they are. With so little moonlight, they're easy to miss. This won't take but a few minutes, Mrs. Maguire. Then I'm anxious to take a sighting on Mars. It should show up with good resolution from where we are and in this light. If you've not seen a planetary surface, you're in for a thrill. Mars has a compelling topography—surface. Like channels. We are not ready to accept that people live there without better evidence, but it's fascinating when magnified."

Seabring continued to mutter and mumble to himself as he maneuvered his telescope on a traversing search of the darkened plains on either side of the Southern and Central right-of-way.

"The tracks are fairly plain, even in the dim night light," he explained, not diverting his attention from his work. "I am scouting approximately a mile on either side of that line. By elevating my tube one click for each pass, I manage an overlapping swath. I know that all sounds hopelessly scientific and complicated to you, Mrs. Maguire."

"Not at all, Dr. Seabring. I'm fascinated already."

"Charming, charming," Seabring muttered to himself, continuing to manipulate his telescope knobs. "If Bodene's gang is out there, I'll find . . . Hello! What's this?" he exclaimed.

Through the dark, Bertha saw Dr. Seabring's spare, scientist's frame, cloaked in his long tan duster, stiffen and become as agitated as a grasshopper cocking its legs to spring.

"Aha! A night fire? Several. Hmm. Must be. Let me bring that a little bit . . ." Seabring hunched closer to his eyepiece with undivided attention, fiddling with another knob, his intent voice no louder than a whisper. Bertha leaned nearer to him, hands propped on knees, watching, drawn in by the suspense.

"That's better. Just now a little more," Seabring said softly. "Resolution. Improving. A slight . . . bit . . . more. Better! Light levels abysmally weak. Looks like . . . three separate fires! Fine-tune focus . . . men moving about. But that's it, by Jove! There it is! Cole called it almost precisely!"

He stepped back with a triumphant grunt. "Huh! As if by Fate or Kismet arranged! Would you care to have a look, Mrs. Maguire? I stake my reputation that we have our device bracketed on Mr. Bodene's night camp!"

"We have!?" she said. "Hadn't we better warn Cole?"

Seabring chuckled. "All in good time, dear lady. All in good time. I'm certain he'll also want to see this. You see, there is no great danger. Have a look. We have found the outlaw camp, but it is on the order of fifty kilometers or perhaps thirty-five miles east. If you care to have a look, you'll think it closer than our camp down there at the slough! I must record in my journal the clarity of the atmosphere at this location. It is phenomenal!"

Seabring stepped aside to allow her to view his find with the pompous air of a king welcoming a distinguished regent to the royal throne room.

"Close one eye and look through the eyepiece, Mrs. Maguire. Be careful not to jostle the instrument; the focus and settings are critically established. A variation by as much as a fraction of a degree, and I might have to hunt half the night to find them again."

Bertha gingerly approached the great telescope and carefully fixed one open eye to the viewing tube. Her vision instantly shrunk down to what seemed to be a three- to four-inch circle. Within that field of view, she clearly saw three night fires and a body of men crouched around them or moving about. Only silence flawed the sensation that she was within a hundred yards of the enemy camp.

"They have weapons and horses, Dr. Seabring," she said, not moving from her position at the telescope. "A man on horseback with a rifle just moved in front of the closest fire."

"Marvelous!" Seabring enthused, standing a few

steps behind her, clutching his lapel in professorial pride. "An equine occultation."

"I'm sorry," she said, misunderstanding, still retaining her absorbed position at the telescope's eyepiece.

Seabring chuckled. "Scientific terminology for a horse moving in front of a fire," he explained.

"How far away are they, did you say, Doctor?"

"I estimate forty-eight to fifty kilometers. Thirty to thirty-five miles by your reference, Mrs. Maguire. Certainly nothing to constitute to us a threat this night, and surely plenty of time tomorrow for Cole and Cap to meditate on their logistics."

"I don't see anybody there that looks like Mr. Smith."

"Umh!" Seabring grunted, coming alert to that reality. "Hadn't thought of that. Excuse me, Mrs. Maguire. That's a critical point. Let me back at the instrument."

As she stepped aside, Seabring said, "On second thought, if you feel you can find your way back to camp, have the others come up. At least Marshal Ryerson. Assure them they have this night no fears of attack by Bad-Face Ike. I'll try for a more critical focus to see if Spunky—Mr. Smith—is their captive."

Seabring waited a fretful hour in the dark of the half acre of tableland; he was anxious for Ryerson to view his distant find before sweeping the heavens for a close look at Mars.

He paced up and down in controlled patience before he heard them quartering up the mesa's slope.

Bertha was in the lead over the trail she'd already covered several times.

The minute he recognized Seabring's figure in the dark and the nearly parallel long gleaming brass telescopic tube, Ryerson vaulted out of the saddle and dropped the reins to ground-tie Jo Shelby.

"You found 'em, Hans. I had a hunch you would," Ryerson cheered as he strode up through the night to the telescope.

"I don't think they've got Spunky, Cole," Seabring said. "I can make out men moving around. They're but vague silhouettes. It's a great distance. They'd have Spunky tied up, and just about every one of them has moved since I began observing. Have a look."

"If he ain't there, then he's either dead or a long ways off. Wish to hell I knew which." Ryerson stepped to the eyepiece. He was just enough taller than both Seabring and Bertha that he had to hunch over slightly to take his sight.

"Damn!" he said, squinting one eye to peer down the magnifying tube. "Clear as a bell! You say it's thirty miles?"

"On that order," Seabring answered.

"The marvels of modern science! What won't they come up with next?! Damn if it doesn't look like I could pick 'em off with a Winchester from here! Did you see Bodene?"

"No way of telling at this distance, Cole. About all I can tell you is there seems to be about the right enough number to be Bad-Face Ike's gang. And they've got guns and horses."

"Bertha told me. What baffles me is where the hell Ike got 'em. But give Ike credit. He's a pretty imaginative cuss. Unless he went all the way to Deep Purple Falls . . . oh, God!"

"What's that, Cole?" Bertha asked.

Ryerson's voice fell, his tone ominous. "Maybe that's what happened to Spunky. A first-class calamity in Al Bumpshas's town!"

"Al . . . huh?" Seabring exclaimed.

"Bumpshas," Ryerson responded. "Hell of a name, I grant you. Southern and Central's kingpin for the Central Division. Sawed-off runt of a man. Just about everybody there and up and down the line jumps through Al Bumpshas's hoop. Al and I aren't on the best of terms, and the love light sure as hell wasn't rekindled if Bodene treed his town."

"So what's our next step, Cole?" Seabring asked.

Ryerson looked at Bertha Maguire, standing beside him in the dense dark close to the land. "It's not going to be easy."

Bertha stiffened. "Cole Ryerson! Don't you dare suggest what's on your mind. I ride with you and the others."

"I just don't think tomorrow's going to be healthy for a woman. Spunky's gone. I hope only lost or befuddled somewhere. But that means five of us— counting you, Bertha—take on Bodene's eighteen. And I'm not prepared to turn back."

"I'll not retreat either, Cole Ryerson."

Ryerson was silent a long moment, thinking. "Huh! I didn't suspect you would. Well . . . you faced 'em down once and saved all our scalps. So it'll ill behoove me to oppose you, Bertha. Just know that it won't be easy."

He turned to Seabring. "Hans, I've seen enough of Ike's camp. You can go back to your stars and moons. Bertha, you and I'd better get back down to camp and get caught up on our rest. Tomorrow's likely to be rougher than rocks in your bed."

17

For all his talk about a good night's sleep, Cole Ryerson lay restless and fretful, the burden of command and decision heavier and more complicated than anything he had faced in years. If, indeed, he must be awake, he'd picked a fine night for it; he studied on that glorious part of his wakefulness from flat on his back, snug in his bedroll, his ceiling a clear, black, and open sky. The awesome dense canopy over him was brilliant, as though speckled and dusted with pure shimmering gold, those silent, distant night companions to a lonely man on the trackless prairie, or like him, a man with a head full of questions and quandaries. In good times and bad, they were a familiar, comforting presence to a man troubled or lonely—or rejoicing in the high feeling of freedom afforded by a night under the stars far from the cares of a mundane, humdrum existence.

Ryerson ached for sleep, but it wasn't in him. The

questions were too ponderous, the decisions too elusive.

"Here you are, Cole Ryerson," he thought, talking to himself, "pushing well past the fifty mark, scalp still intact. Maybe already you're too old for this ridiculous nonsense. Bodene has guns and horses. Al Bumpshas's people didn't just give all that stuff away, so no doubt there are dead men in Deep Purple Falls. That'll make Ike all the more desperate. At last count, eighteen rode with him. Pitiful odds."

Ryerson sighed and continued to contemplate the host of stars arrayed like a silent symphony for the eyes. And for the soul. Awed by their magnificence, he imagined he could almost hear organ music. Though the vista should have eased him, his mind worked and worried back over his difficulties like a creek fretting its way down a twisty, rocky bed. A soft breeze cooled and helped comfort and soothe him; that was a blessing.

"Some time tomorrow I face his pack of wolves with three men and a woman, all as cast-iron fearless as they come, but their dependability as fighters, well . . . who's to say? I could be leading them to their deaths . . . as well as my own. Besides, our maneuverability is hopelessly burdened by eighteen borrowed swaybacks that I've signed for. For now, I'm stuck with 'em. Such a mess!"

Ryerson closed his eyes, determined to concentrate on sleep. In spite of himself, the lids clicked open again, and he asked his friends the stars, "What the hell happened to Spunky?"

Ryerson knew he had slept at least a short time when pale blue light filtered through his eyelids and he woke to a gray dawn. Though he'd slept, he didn't feel at all rested.

He raised up and disentangled himself from his soogans with their ground cloth and top cover. He slid out to perch on the still-warm rumpled mess. Uncharacteristically, he abruptly fished in his gear for his cigarette makin's, built a smoke, and sat watching the huddled sleeping forms of his four companions, now mere lumps of bulky and grimy canvas ducking bedroll covers under the beginning light of daybreak.

Ryerson rarely smoked before his morning coffee and most often not until he'd finished his breakfast. This morning it was a quiet comfort to a mind that still hadn't straightened out the snags and snarls it went to bed with. He sat, knees drawn up and loosely circled by his arms, mind still churning, his crude cigarette parked between his fingers. He let it burn and allowed his mind to idle on the day. The softly billowing plume of tobacco smoke, blue in the growing light from the east, entranced and fascinated him with its myriad of tiny swirling currents and clouds in the still, calm air of dawn.

Strange, he thought, how little things like that could ease a troubled mind. They did nothing to provide a decision, but maybe the relaxation to his thought process might let in a little light. His mind drifted back to it, his problems suddenly jabbed with a reality that all that woolgathering hadn't accomplished a thing.

He angrily and bitterly tossed the stained, soggy butt into the firepit and abruptly stood up, tall against the sky.

He grabbed the big speckled enamel coffeepot that

clanked loudly on its rusted, deformed bail and headed for a spot of clear water in the slough. It was time.

"All right!" he yelled, gruff as a sergeant major. "Out of your rolls and sun your souls! We probably got a fight to fight this day, and the sooner we get at it, the sooner we get out of it!"

Sleepy, startled and tousled heads popped like jack-in-the-boxes from under four bedroll covers arrayed like spokes of a wheel, feet toward their rock-edged fire ring.

For the first time, he noticed that Bertha had cloaked her head and tied-up hair under a domed and gray heavy wool knit nightcap to ward off the cold. Beyond her sometimes maddening thoroughness, she was a practical planner. How many bitterly cold camp nights he could remember yearning for something of the kind, but such a quick, easy solution had never occurred to him.

Ryerson called a formation before they reluctantly quit their pleasant campsite under the cottonwoods. Reviewing them like a company commander, he mentally marveled and shuddered at his troop. It wasn't much, but it was a hell of a lot, and he swelled with pride. A wisp of a scientist in long linen duster, bullet-riddled straw hat and little windowpanes bridging his nose, clutching the reins close to the bit to control his horse. Beside Hans, hatless, his full and silver white topknot a-gleam in the sun, stood the seventy-four-year-old and seamy-faced Cap Donovan, once pride of the Texas Rangers; granite tough as any Alamo defender, Cap would take out his share before they got ball or blade into him. Bertha Maguire, gritty

208

in slouch hat and tan canvas, corduroy-collared trail coat buttoned to the throat, sparking eyes fierce and determined as any man's. Wiry and forced-lean Fernando, also hatless, in worn, probably cast-off clothing, his thick straight obsidian hair glinting flintlike in the sun, his naturally umber skin almost as black from a life in the open.

"Folks," Ryerson began. "I promised you—except you weren't there, Bertha—when we started this dance that I intended to capture Ike Bodene for the last time. He's out there now, within thirty miles of our position, unquestionably headed our way, still out to get me and anybody that stands with me. He's armed and he's mounted and probably more out for blood than ever."

Ryerson fixed a sparking squint on his squad. "As already overwhelmed as we are, I'll still not back away from this one. This at last is *degüello,* the fight to the last man. No quarter given. To the death! Bodene either dies, surrenders, or rides over us."

Ryerson paused a long time; the hours since he peeked through Dr. Seabring's telescope at Ike's gang had brought no solutions. Still, he knew what he had to do, face it, one step at a time, with Ryerson's Renegades or without them. He spoke with as much resolve as he could muster.

"Each of you has the choice, and I mean this without burdening anyone with shame or guilt. Anyone without the stomach to face death before dinnertime may ride on out now."

He paused further, studying them, his eyes a gem glint out of an equally determined face. No one moved.

"This is my fight," he continued. "When it all shakes out, it's not yours. Bad-Face Ike is after me. Not you. I face him on whatever terms he and the conditions dictate. You owe me nothing. Save your necks, for God's sake! Ride on! Now!"

The four beside their horses in line in front of him froze to more of a rock-firm, stubborn, unmoving military attention, eyes resolutely fixed on his. No one looked at the others for wavering or weakness or to see who might break out of line first to take the offer and be the one to follow away from Ryerson's grim challenge.

Ryerson waited and watched, seeing not a flicker of indecision.

"All right, damn fools! We ride to capture Ike Bodene. He's south of the tracks, headed this way. Fernando, you're our spearhead that way, at point, our forward eyes. The instant you spot them, get back to the so-called main body so we take defensive, offensive, diversionary, or precautionary measures, *sabe, hombre?*"

The depth in Fernando's unwavering black eyes was unmistakable; he got it.

"Cap Donovan, you ride north of the line, to our left, off maybe a hundred yards into the chaparral; scan your area for any sign of Spunky. Hans, Bertha, and I will travel close to center, eastbound following the railway.

"Now. If contact is made, Cap, immediately report back to me. We'll head for the Timberlodge slopes, fighting a rearguard action until I can find us a defensible hillside position where they can't reach or flank us and we can direct our fire down on them. And hope we locate ourselves so we can't be cut off or harassed from the rear in any event. I just hope such tactical terrain can be found under duress. Huh!"

"What's that, Cole?"

"I was thinking about old Custer and taking the high ground, which he did. Obedient to Rogers. Only trouble was the Sioux flanked him, took higher ground, and cut off his escape hatch. Rogers's Twelfth Commandment. And what may save us if we get into a real scrap with Bodene." Ryerson recited it, almost by rote. "'If you determine to rally after a retreat in order to make a fresh stand against the enemy, by all means endeavor to do it on the most rising ground you come at, which will give you greatly the advantage in the point of situation, and enable you to repulse superior numbers.'"

Ryerson turned silent.

"What's the matter, Cole?" Donovan asked.

"I was just thinking. All this begins to sound like Old Testament prophecy."

Bertha straightened, more alert. "Prithee explain "

Cole studied her. "If we ride out unscathed from a certain-death situation because of hundred-year-old backwoods fighting savvy, wouldn't you begin to believe it justifies the Scriptures?"

"Let's think about that when we've won the day, Cole," Donovan insisted. "Like you always say, let's take it one step at a time. Now it's time to take the first step."

"Right, Cap," Ryerson said, rousing out of deep thought. "Any questions, anybody?"

Fernando regarded him curiously. "What about me, Meester Ryerson?"

"That's all in the plan, Fernando. Get away from them as fast as you can after you report to me. Ride for Deep Purple Falls. It's a hell of a ways, *amigo*. You'd better take a spare mount on your scout. As fast as you can, find the telegrapher at the Southern and Central station. Wire Major Fred C. Locke at Camp Walker of our situation and position and to send help. It will be too late, but at least what's left of us may be found before the buzzards and the coyotes get to work. And for whatever it's worth by that time, try to find Spunky."

Ryerson paused again to think about small details. "If we're attacked, Bertha and Hans, we stampede the horse herd back toward the enemy. They are such habitual horse thieves, they may be tempted at least to slow down. That diversion could buy us a little more time to find a proper place to fort up.

"Everything else is too sketchy to even discuss. We'll meet each step head-on and use our best judgment. And . . . thanks to all of you for sticking by me."

He studied the line of the surviving Ryerson's Renegades one last time, feeling his eyes growing a bit misty. He whacked his thigh with his hat, yelling lustily, "Let's ride!"

18

*

With a happy, cavalier wave and broad grin, Fernando rode off to scout Ike's movement out south toward Timberlodge while Cap Donovan's silver white hair disappeared into the chaparral and malpais to the north of the rail line. Guiding the horses, Ryerson, Bertha, and Seabring veered away from the tracks about twenty-five yards, eastward bound, each silently alert, minds focused at one point—to expect the unexpected; the startling, shocking moment of encounter could come at any time.

East was about to meet west, with stunning—if not fatal—catastrophe as a distinct possibility.

Ryerson asked Bertha to ride drag on the horse herd while he and Seabring kept the leaders pointed east. "With all due respect to your admirable strengths and skills, Mrs. Maguire," he said, "but with deference to your femininity, I'd feel more secure if you'd allow Hans and me to ride forward."

"Permission granted, Mr. Ryerson," Bertha an-

213

swered sweetly. "Just swing wide when the shooting starts, for I intend to be up there to cut a considerable swath with John's Winchester."

In a sudden burst of new amazement at the woman's guts, Ryerson glanced at Seabring to plumb the scientist's reaction. His face was wreathed in an "I-could-have-told-you-so, Cole" grin.

Ryerson's chest filled. The spare-framed Seabring at the last minute had girded for war. Gone was the linen laboratory smock, gone the peculiar little spectacles, gone the low-crowned, gunshot straw hat. His full head of blondish, hair rippled in the morning breeze, his long-sleeved crisp white shirt partly cloaked by a European-style leather jerkin.

The menacing blued steel barrel of his custom Sharps, butt plate on thigh, right hand gripping fore end, pointed skyward like a stubby Prussian lance without pennon, its lock plate, hammer, and breech a rainbow swirl of gleaming, case-hardened colors.

His eyes darting, occupied with searching the barren, sprawling wasteland ahead for any sign of oncoming movement, Ryerson again marveled in a tiny recess of his brain at his small but stubbornly valiant band.

Perhaps, he thought, when the battle was joined, Fernando and Cap—in true Rogers's Regulations fashion—would drive in Ike's flankers to bring chaos to the enemy's main body. He and his meager force charging Ike's center might exploit the confusion and decimate them sufficiently to rout the gang to a speedy capitulation.

They drove the horses for an uneventful twenty minutes, stoically vigilant, a respectable distance apart with their horse herd duties. Around them the land changed almost imperceptibly, cut here and there by ever-deepening washes and draws, developing into country of slow downslopes and gradual rises, upthrust outcroppings and hidden pockets.

"Good terrain for an ambush," Ryerson guardedly warned Seabring riding across the herd from him. "Stay doubly sharp."

The scientist grimly acknowledged with a look and a nod.

In a deep gravel swale dense with ground-hugging sagebrush and spiky cholla, Ryerson, growing more concerned with the hazardous nature of the region, brought up his hand for a halt, waved Bertha forward, and began circling the horses. As she approached, he started to move close enough to suggest that as they move out they space themselves even farther apart to make smaller targets through this broken, craggy land.

Movement on the hilltop ahead brought up three pairs of eyes to abruptly lock on the darkened outline of a man staggering to the brow of the hill, his swaying form starkly backlit by the early morning sun.

"Jesus!" Ryerson grunted in sudden alarm. Despite his projecting hat brim, he whipped up his hand to shield his eyes against the glaring sunlight. "Holy Hell! It's Fernando!"

"Lord in Heaven!" Bertha gasped.

Fernando wavered on unsteady legs on the graveled crest above them. He was shirtless, his torso a carmined mass of blood and crisscrossed with knife slashes or welts from the lash of a bullwhip.

He stiffly brought up both arms to painfully wave them off. "Meester Ryerson!" The feeble, cracking voice drifted down to them. "Go back! Go back!" The supreme effort of his strained words cut into their guts like a driven knife.

A barrage of nearby rifles behind him roared in thunderous volley, and Fernando's body leaped, jerked, and spun as bullets slammed into him with spattering sprays of blood and torn flesh. His body was impelled forward; enough control remained for him to make five leaping downslope strides. His knees buckled and he plummeted forward, landing on the side of his head and shoulder in a ragged somersault and then to pitch, slide, and roll sidewise nearly at their feet.

Ryerson was off Jo Shelby and at Fernando's side in an instant. The upturned grimy, sweated, contorted face relaxed with the approach of death, his eyes closed, his lips struggling over words that didn't come.

"It's okay, Fernando," Ryerson assured. "Okay now. You're back with us." He raised hopeless, helpless eyes at Bertha and Seabring.

"Ike he catch me," Fernando whispered hoarsely, thick crimson blood bubbles popping on his lips. "Beat up. Cut me. Send me walking. Maybe you come out, help, and Ike could kill. But I show summabitch . . . yell to go away. I pretty damn good Renegade, Meester Ryerson?"

"You damn betcha, Fernando," Ryerson assured heartily, hoping he could hear. He knew he did when a strained grin stretched the blood ruby lips. The young Mexican's thin smile relaxed, and he was dead.

Ryerson leaped up and rudely grabbed Fernando's legs by the ankles to skid the body away to the side.

"Cole!" Seabring shrieked. "What in hell are you doing?!"

"Gettin' 'im out of the gawdam way!" Ryerson bellowed back hoarsely in high passion. The only course left was a bold, aggressive frontal assault on Bodene's line. His teeth-gritted words totally ignored Bertha's feminine sensibilities. "We'll come back for 'im. Paint for a gawdam cavalry charge without troopers but with a hell of a lot of horses! Christ, wisht I had a gawdam saber! Hans! Bertha! Spread them horses out. Broad front!"

Bertha and Seabring watched him, listening attentively.

"This is it!" Ryerson continued. "No time. Stampede the horses. Split up and rout Ike as best we can. We all got to take out six men each. Make every shot count. I don't care how many times you're hit. Count for your six! Ike'll be on us in a minute. Got to move!"

From their left, from the north, hugging his horse's neck while their hearts leaped, in a thunder of hooves and a cloud of dust, Cap Donovan galloped in under a hail of bullets, his silver hair now encased in what appeared to be Spunky's old hat. That absurdity in such a desperate moment made Ryerson want to burst out laughing.

"Where in the hell'd you get that hat?"

"Spunky's," Cap yelled breathlessly. "Found it yonder by the tracks."

Ryerson quickly recovered. "No time for chitchat," he bellowed. "We move out against Ike. Fernando's dead, Cap."

"Shit!" Donovan responded.

"The horses are our element of surprise. Each of us take out five, at least four. Survivors head south into the Timberlodge hills! Make a stand. High ground. Follow me. Let's go!"

Their prancing, riderless horses spread along a wide front, the four gallant defenders racing along with them, urging them forward at the gallop, Ryerson's Renegades poured bravely up and out of the hollow, crested the summit and charged, driving the thundering horses across a flat stretch; in the distance, ranked in a military-like front formation came the imposing and sinister dark line of the Bodene gang, Winchesters and Colts ineffectively popping rounds their way.

Ryerson surmised that a handful of Bodene's men had prodded Fernando to the rim of the deep draw in a planned ambush; Fernando's insolence earned him a close-range firing squad.

Over the din of almost a hundred pounding hooves, Ryerson continued to roar hoarse commands to charge at the gallop. He gripped the wrist of his old reliable Winchester carbine in much the same fashion as a familiar cavalry saber, muzzle thrust forward saberlike, aimed at the enemy, the Winchester's lever loop like a saber's brass basket guard. "Charge 'em!" he shrieked. "All horns and rattles! Them chili-eatin' drizzlebutts can't score a hit on us for dry owl shit!"

Involuntarily, the old rebel yell rose like renewed courage and daring in his maddened throat; the onrushing outlaws were still a hundred yards out.

Galloping ahead of the thunder and the dust like a spirit from memorable charges of a long-lost past leading his command by several horse lengths Ryerson's heart raced with the familiar, throat

scraping raucous screech building in his lungs. And in
his loins. Newtonia. Helena. Pea Ridge. With General
Shelby. It all swirled back as fiercely as the whirlwind
whips its fury; the well-remembered stark clash,
crunch, and concussion—the splendor and the sting
—of combat reemerged out of the mists of time and
place. Lips parted, his jaw dropped and he released it
again down the years in all the glory for which it
stood; a mighty clarion call to uncommon valor.

"EEEeeee-YYYooowwhh!"

Around him, brittle and seasoned old U.S. cavalry
chargers turned bold with the thrilling summons to
greatness and picked up the shriek with neighs and
fearsome trumpeting. Bertha, Cap, and Seabring
heard it and clawed breath into their lungs and belted
out the screech as they closed the gap and closed ranks
behind Ryerson.

Reprising the lusty yell, he trained his practiced eye
at the onrushing horde in these precious, dramatic
seconds before the clash; Ike was poorly horsed,
poorly armed. Six outlaws raced at him on foot, some
firing Winchesters, but more with limited range
sidearms. Of Ike's eighteen, a mere dozen were
mounted. Ryerson rejoiced; his prospects brightened
by the moment. He lifted his voice again in the
magnificent, defiant rebel yell.

Taken by surprise at the thundering phalanx of
horses rising like a legion of hell-sent demons out of
the land ahead and the Satanic screeches of men and
horses, Ike's line wavered.

Bellowing the blood-chilling shriek the loudest
from the tip of the ragged flying wedge of plummeting
horseflesh, Ryerson appeared invincible as again and

again Bodene's riflemen snapped shots in his direction.

Ike's riders and gunmen afoot broke and scattered as the broad front of stampeding horses slammed into them, unhorsing several startled riders; stirrups flapping, the errant saddle horses joined the stampede away from the milling outlaws.

Riding into the jumbled mass, Ryerson picked his targets carefully, judging the riders as the most strategic; a man knocked out of the saddle left a spooked horse to bolt away. Near him in the confusing chaos of men, horses and the peppering bursts of gunfire, a dusky rider under a roof of steeple sombrero with a canvas bandolier of fat cartridges across his chest took menacing aim at him with a big-bore Winchester.

Ryerson one-handed his little lever-action carbine like a pistol to pop the man out of the saddle before he could get off the first round. An outlaw bullet from somewhere whacked Ryerson's tall Stetson, sending it galley west.

Then they were beyond Ike's line, thundering away into the desert, the stampeding horse herd disappearing down the chaparral ahead of them; the horses were a lost cause, Ryerson judged, swinging Jo Shelby back to rejoin the fracas.

Around him, rifles popping, Bertha, Cap, and Seabring swung and sashayed their mounts like true horse soldiers, giving good accounting of themselves as they took on the superior force of Ike's outlaws.

Christ! Ryerson thought impulsively, and I questioned their fighting abilities. He felt the jerk of a bullet tear through the flapping skirt of his broadcloth coat. As his close-by assailant feverishly jacked a fresh round into the chamber, Ryerson forced Jo Shelby next to the man, viciously jammed the carbine's muzzle into his midsection and fired. "There, you son of a bitch!" Ryerson screeched; gleaming ruby and terra-cotta guts spilled over the saddle horn as the man's abdominal cavity was blown wide open by the ferocious muzzle blast of the point-blank charge. The mortally wounded rider drooped, strangely limp and leaning sidewise like a rag doll in the saddle as his spine, shattered by the departing mushroomed .44/40 slug, yielded its support.

In a hasty, judgmental survey, Ryerson saw that his advantage of surprise had been quickly lost; Ike's ranks regrouped, reformed their line, the flankers guiding it into a menacing semicircle that would fast become a surround.

"Cap!" he screamed at the old hellion fighting like a Trojan near him, knowing Bertha and Seabring would hear as well. "Sound retreat! Take the high ground. Follow me!"

Bareheaded, damning the son of a bitch that knocked his hat off, Ryerson wheeled Jo Shelby a hundred and eighty degrees and drove out of Bodene's threatening encirclement, his three unscathed Renegades close on his tail, pursued by Ike's dwindling band of horsemen, valiantly snapping shots back over their shoulders as they fled the skirmish.

Ike's now-ineffective foot soldiers—increased by several riders whose horses had deserted under fire—raggedly loped and lagged into the dust cloud churned up as Ike's mounted handful gave merry chase to the quartet of Ryerson's Renegades.

Pivoting his body to pop another handheld shot at the pursuers, Ryerson's quick count put nine of Ike's gang on horseback; the odds had evened fast.

Spinning his attention back to the fast-rising land ahead, he spied a boulder-strewn slope that would offer plenty of cover; the protective butte behind it would be virtually inaccessible for Ike to send up snipers to fire down on them from the rimrock.

"Hans! Bertha!" he yelled. "The high rocks! Yonder! Forget the horses. Grab your canteens. Fort up! Give as good as you get!"

They veered slightly in their race to the craggy sanctuary. With Jo Shelby under him narrowing the gap to the rocks, Ryerson grimaced; Ike had him by the balls again. At least the defensive position would buy his pitiful Renegades a little more time.

Walking the Southern and Central railroad ties westward from Deep Purple Falls, a thin, moth-eaten blanket clutched under his arm like a hobo's bindle, a troubled Spunky Smith mused that the Sewer and Cesspool must have deliberately spaced their damned ties to make walking extremely awkward. He was not yet fully out of the switch yards when he spied his salvation.

On a siding perched a low-slung, short-gaited two-man handcar, a man-powered, cam-operated pumper device with waist-high horizontal oak bars polished smooth from considerable use by greasy palms. One desperate man might make the damned thing work.

Fleetingly, he wondered if handcar theft carried the same penalty as horse thievery. Instead of seeing him hanged, Al Bumpshas would most likely make him sign another bogus invoice.

He looked around. No one in sight. No eyewitnesses to the crime. He tossed the coiled blanket ahead of him, carefully laying his Winchester down, stepped up to the weathered plank deck, and tested the device's action.

It worked smoothly with only a soft purr of the four small flanged wheels coursing over the track. The switch was open, and he pumped his steed out onto the main line.

Again westward bound at a comforting rate of speed, the wind drying his sweaty hair, Spunky only hoped that Al Bumpshas was right that there'd be no train traffic on the line for several days.

19

———◆———

Time took the night off as Spunky pumped the handcar through the endless, dense darkness, exhausted but driven to reunite with Ryerson's Renegades. He stayed constantly—and cautiously—alert to overtaking Bodene's gang along these very tracks; they were ahead of him by little more than two hours, many of their horses slowed by carrying double loads. The handcar's speed, he figured, was something better than Ike's bunch would do. He was on edge all night.

Morning came up gray behind him. As features on the land took form out of dawn's mists, he found nothing familiar. His shoulders and arms rebelling against eternal exertion, he caught his breath and resumed his race with the westbound sun.

Hours later, the sun warming the back of his neck, over the soft whir of polished cams and flanged wheels, he harkened to the muted pop of distant gunfire; the handcar rolled on its own as his ears sought to better define the approaching sound.

Sure enough, he thought with alarm; Ryerson and the Bodene bunch must be mixing it up. At the moment, he had little notion what he could do to help; just get there and take what came.

Abruptly, almost too far to see, men on foot, mere distant specks, crossed the tracks to the south side and disappeared into the chaparral. Heat and distance created the illusion that they floated out there on a film of sky blue water.

He waited while the handcar slowly coasted toward a gradual stop. He resumed a cautious pumping of the handle, easing his way along the tracks to get closer to the action; as he coaxed his conveyance westward, the sounds of rifle fire grew in their intensity. Spunky's heart pounded; Ryerson's Renegades were pinned down somewhere south, fighting for their lives.

He struggled with feelings of urgency for sudden, reckless and heedless action; dead, he'd be little help to Cole. As close now as he felt he could be on the handcar, he let it glide to a stop of its own momentum and slipped off easily to the slag roadbed. He carefully lifted one corner to test its heft; it took brawn but rose heavily under his hands. It would be easier for two men. In a few minutes of grunting work, he had it safely pried off to the side of the tracks. Grabbing his Winchester and checking for a full magazine tube, he left the mangy blanket roll and set off diagonally across the desert toward the sounds of sporadic gunfire. To hell, he thought, with Al Bumpshas and his precious blanket; if he never saw the sawed-off runt again, it would be too soon.

For nearly an hour Spunky hiked the broken country, his fatigue and grinding muscle cramps set aside in his need to hurl himself into the midst of the Renegades' desperate situation. The countryside made for rough going, sloping up toward Timberlodge and broken with washes and outcroppings to slog through or veer around.

He paused to rest a moment in the bottom of a draw, to take a breather and to give relief to rebelling muscles; he knelt on one knee, partly supporting himself with his vertical gun barrel. He lowered his head and briefly closed his eyes.

"Hold it right there, mister!" came a bark from behind him, and Spunky was instantly alert, careful not to make any rash moves. His heart sank; he'd violated a cardinal commandment of backwoods survival that predated even Ryerson's precious Rogers's Regulations—he hadn't watched his back trail.

"Ain't goin' nowhere," Spunky declared, weighing his words, still kneeling, keeping the Winchester's muzzle skyward, his eyes straight ahead. "Whatcha want?"

"You ain't no Mex or Injun," the man said. "Turn around."

Spunky slowly lifted and pivoted his head to come nearly face-to-face with old Dave Nesler!

"Wait a minute!" Nesler blurted. "You're one 'em deputies ridin' with old Boot Hill after Buckshot Bob or whatever his name is that killed my Sal!"

"Bad-Face Ike," Spunky corrected. "And you're Dave Nesler. What're you doing way out here?"

"Why, headed back to my claim when I heard tha: fracas commencin' this mornin' and snuck up for a look-see. I see a bunch of them *comancheros* wearin out boot leather up to'ard the hills and figured to folle:

'em. I seen you get off that little railway cart down the line an' trailed you up here, too. What's goin' on?"

"Glad you're here, Dave," Spunky said. "Cole right now probably needs all the help he can get. But you went to Fort Walker weeks ago."

Nesler shrugged self-consciously. "Reckon I went on a toot in town. An' you know how that'll make a man lose track of days. Hard to bear for a while, thinkin' of goin' back there without Sal."

"Well," Spunky said. "You got your rifle and I got mine. We'd best get up there and see what can be done to help Cole."

Nesler was thoughtful a long moment. "I don't look it now, mister, but I rode as cap'n under General John Bell Hood, CSA, in the late unpleasantness. I learnt a thing or two. We're comin' up from the rear, you an' me. Good position to harass the foe. You take left flank, I'll take right. Them scallywags'll be pretty much in a straight line facin' Boot Hill's emplacement an' won't figure on rearguard action. Find you a hidey hole yonder on the left to where your rifle's sighted in proper to their line. Remember that. You got to be dead on with your sights. No misses or our fat's in the fire. Keep low.

"When they git to shootin' up a storm, pick off the man farthest left. Make sure you drill 'im proper an' jest keep doin' that, workin' inward. That way you don't sound the alarm too soon that those rascals are departin' to eternity in wholesale lots. Stay down in between shots. Got to let 'em think Boot Hill's bunch is doin' the fancy shootin' even if they come to and see that a passel of their pards is already dead, which I 'spect they won't till too late."

227

"Kill 'em all?" Spunky asked.

"If that's what it takes to save your pards. Speck Face'll fly the white flag long 'fore that. He's the one I want. I aim to dry his skulp tacked to my cabin door!"

"Cole won't let you do that, Nesler!"

"A lot he's got to say. I'm the one's going to save his mountain oysters in a few minutes. Let's march."

"I ain't moving," Spunky protested. "I ain't going to let you shoot Bad-Face Ike without justifiable cause."

"Aw, hell," Nesler confessed suddenly. "I guess I ain't going to do that anyways. Was a time I would've. That larrup in town kinda took the edge off my mad. Guess I've gone soft."

"I'll get you a front-row seat at his hangin'."

Nesler stared at Spunky wide-eyed. "Think you could do that?!"

"Depend on it. Let's just get up there and get to work."

Without another word, Nesler spun on his heel and stumped away to Spunky's right. "Son of a bitch!" Spunky heard him mutter to himself. "Never been to a hangin'!" He stopped abruptly and turned back.

"Oh, hey! Meant to tell you. Found a hell of a mess this mornin' yonder across the line. In one of them gullies. That Mex jasper you rode with, you and Boot Hill. Somebody'd sliced him up right proper with a sharp butcher knife. Then looked like he'd been backshot eight, ten times, every which way. Even had a few rounds in 'is ass. Poor bastard sure died hard."

Spunky pursed his lips and clamped his eyes in sudden grief. "Fernando!" he muttered through gritted teeth. He felt himself cut, close to the core.

"There was sign, too," Nesler continued, "of a mess of hosses millin' around and then dug gravel up and out of there. Makes me wonder. What do you make of that?"

Poor Fernando, Spunky thought, never did get to teach him poker. He fought his way back to the here and now.

"By God, Dave, you're full of surprises. Now tell me. You didn't see any other *messes* over that way, did you?"

"No! What'd you expect?"

Spunky found himself fired with a bitter drive for revenge. First Cactus Jack and now Fernando. For a moment, he thought that Nesler's notion of tacking Bad-Face Ike's scalp to his cabin door was a capital idea. Then he remembered what he was there for. "We better get busy up yonder, Dave, and make sure Bodone doesn't create any more messes out of Ryerson's posse."

Nesler made a jerking motion with his rifle's muzzle to the left motioning him that way. Spunky brought his Winchester to the ready and stepped off boldly. Now and then in his quartering advance to his left, he saw Nesler picking his way far to the right, ever forward. He was glad the old prospector had showed up, and that they'd made a sound plan.

The resounding peals of gunfire grew in intensity and harshness as Spunky eased forward, favoring the east, searching for his sniper's nest. The land was grooved with washes and spiked with lofty outcroppings on the way up to Timberlodge as he picked his way slowly toward the action.

To his left a tortured and rifted mesa rose, its

backside of sloping talus manageable. He struggled to its summit to peer down on the fighting.

In the swale below, he had a clear view of about fourteen of Bodene's survivors behind the excellent cover of giant boulders. Upslope another seventy-five yards, Ryerson's Renegades had forted up, backs to a sheer precipice, themselves firing from protective high rocks.

Urgency driving him, he wiggled himself and his Winchester into a man-sized flatbedded fracture in the rimrock, inching forward to take a commanding view of the scene below from the cover of a squat, shielding juniper. He raised his head above the rock to his right to try for a glimpse of Nesler; the old prospector must have found his spot. A head poked out of the rocks from Ryerson's position to bring a hail of rifle blasts from Bodene's line.

Spunky saw a distant rifleman on Ike's extreme right jerk, convulse, and lie still; Nesler, he surmised, was cutting a fresh notch on his Winchester's fore end. Now it was his turn.

Jesus, he thought in sudden reality; I've never backshot a man! A few had gone under from the close-range spit of his hogleg Colt. But that was different; then they'd faced each other in parity. He could walk away with his head up.

Spunky had always despised backshooters and grifters.

Ah, hell, he thought. A man does what he's got to do when duty calls. He took his squint down the sights laying his bead on the hatband of the man at the far left. Here goes, he thought.

In the midst of the concussion welling up from below, his rifle merely bucked against his shoulder, no sound apparent. His quarry jerked, slumped, and lay quiet as a church mouse.

Spunky drew in a deep, trembling breath to combat the turbulence within.

Curious as he struggled against involuntary spasms of shame, he scanned Bodene's line Nesler's way. Two more lay awkward and silent at their hasty rifle ports; Nesler had gotten ahead of him.

The firing below subsided.

"Ryerson!" Bodene yelled, and the name rose crystal clear as it bounced off mighty monarchs of granite towering over them. "Ready to call it quits? There's no water up there, and if that's not enough, I'll starve you out!"

Ryerson's voiced boomed down at the outlaws, and Spunky thought he'd burst with pride at Cole's audacity.

"Not a chance, Ike! Can't consider it at least before tomorrow noon." Cole's words resounded off the hills with astonishing clarity. "Mrs. Maguire's up here. You remember her. She fixed you some might good chuck on the trail a few days back. Bet you ain't grazed like that since. She's brought a haunch of venison and's fixin' potatoes and beans tonight and some good fresh sourdough bread. In the mornin' we're havin' bakin' powder biscuits and venison gravy! In between, we'll have plenty of good, hot coffee and an ample supply of well-aged corn squeezin's to keep our spirits up for mornin' and evenin' relaxin'. If you ain't got anythin' near that good, maybe you'd ought to consider tuckin' tail yourself, droppin' your guns and comin' on up here to enjoy supper with us. As my Indian brothers say, 'The robe is spread and the pipe is lit.'"

Ryerson paused. "But if that don't scour, Ike, maybe we can talk about surrender after our dinner tomorrow noon. Till then you can just keep on wastin' ca'tridges. We're pretty well fixed up here in the meantime."

With that, Ryerson arrogantly poked his head and his Winchester out from behind a hillside rock and plowed a round downslope. It glanced off Ike's covering rock to whine sharply away into the distance. Spunky could see Ike Bodene making himself small behind his rock.

As the bullet's twang faded far to Spunky's right, another voice boomed with all the magnitude of the Sermon on the Mount.

"Me, now, I ain't waitin' all night and half a day. Ain't as good fixed for grub. Stand up and hold still, Ugly Mug, so's I can put one square through your lights. I aim to even the score for my dog Sal. You got a lot less to crow about since you come up here, Ugly. My pardner yonder and me seen to that! The backshootin' days are over for some of them on your right and left flanks."

Bodene shrank closer to the earth at finding himself totally bluffed as well as surrounded.

Ryerson's voice again rose out of the high rocks shaking with relief and bewilderment. "Who's that? That you, Dave Nesler?"

"It's me," Nesler's bass voice echoed, "and I'm holdin' a bead on old Peck-Face yonder."

"You said pardner," Ryerson's voice rang in the

taut air. "Who's that with you? I have a hunch it's a stouthearted man!"

Jubilantly, Spunky threw back his head, ready to bellow. "Sylvester Smith, Deputy United States Marshal! Coverin' right flank! We can put the rest of 'em under before they catch our scent!"

Ryerson's voice boomed again. "Spunky Smith, by God! Among the living again. Glad you made it out. Okay, how about it, Ike? Ready to call it quits?"

Bitterness tinged the words that bounced off the towering Timberlodge foothill escarpments. "Call off your goddamned dogs, Ryerson! We're whipped."

20

━━◆━━

Cole Ryerson's beefy mitts again clutched the polished mahogany and green felt rim of the billiard table in the back room of McCurdy's Saloon and looked over his stouthearted men—Spunky, Cap, and Hans Seabring. Dave Nesler had gone back to his gold claim on Timberlodge. Bertha declined an invitation to the last get-together of Ryerson's Renegades, pleading the press of getting caught up on long-neglected housekeeping chores.

Behind him, glaring yellow sunlight poked through the dingy tan of the discolored window to make a broad rectangular but hazy shaft of the stirred-up dust within the gray room.

"Well, gents," Ryerson said, "seems like just the other day we assembled here. Of course, a couple of us are missing. But I suppose without getting mushy that they'll be alive in our hearts for years to come. We'll go out to the saloon in a few minutes and

234

hoist a few to the memory of Cactus Jack and Fernando.

"You all got your part of the bounty for the 'dead or alives' from Bad-Face Ike's gang. Bertha has Cactus Jack's share, and I put Fernando's cut in the bank here at compound interest. One of these days soon, I'll ride down El Paso way and go south of the line and try to find his village and his family and let 'em know how gallantly he died. I'm sure they can use the money.

"So things are getting wrapped up in a nutshell. With the murders of Cactus Jack and Fernando, along with butchering those two jaspers in Deep Purple Falls, Judge Winfield's convinced he'll get a hangin' verdict for Ike and the other ten we brought in." Ryerson paused, turning thoughtful; he had brought in Bad-Face Ike for the last time—but at what kind of a cost?

They'd buried Fernando on the bluff where he was shot. Under armed supervision, the remnants of Ike's gang were directed to provide a decent burial for seven of their comrades at the site of the desert skirmish and horse stampede.

"Strange how it all worked out," Ryerson said, stepping back from the table, his burly form a virtual silhouette against the eerie light streaming in the window. "Like everything fell right back in our laps after Ike caved in. That horse herd moseyin' in to join our remuda—the cavalry nags, the ones Ike stole in Deep Purple Falls, and most of them he lost up on Timberlodge in the first place. How horses know to circle up with their kind, maybe for mutual protection

—from miles away—sure does beat all. I tell you, boys, these eyes have seen some queer sights, but wakin' up that mornin' to find our horse herd damned near tripled or better, well, sir, that just about takes the cake.

"Oh, Spunky . . . I notified Al Bumpshas by telegraph that he could claim them twelve mounts at the livery stable corral here in Fort Walker. And pay their keep. He wired back that he's gonna send a couple of stock cars to Coyote Siding and have some boys ride up here and get 'em and give 'em a train ride back to Deep Purple Falls."

"Why tell me all this, Cole?" Spunky asked.

"Well, Bumpshas tacked on a sort of message to you at the end of his wire. Seems you owe him for a blanket and a penalty for unauthorized use of a 'mobile personnel conveyance,' whatever the hell that is. Young Higgins over to the telegraph office had a hell of a time transcribing them words off the Morse Code. Does all that mean anything to you?"

Spunky scowled and growled. "He'll have to hunt me down up on Timberlodge." Then his voice brightened. "Cap and I are going up there with Doc Seabring. I'm gonna build me a log cabin—what you might call a 'timber lodge'—off a ways up there and work up a nice stable and corral for Old Stockholder. Spend my time riding them hills among them inspirin' trees, watchin' the aspens turnin' gold agin the tangy-smellin' green pines, huntin' my winter meat, carin' for my horse, enjoyin' the peace and silence, and workin' for Doc Seabring."

The scientist, looking grand and professorial again in his calf-length linen coat, his battered little straw hat, and his oval spectacles gleaming like mirrors, spoke up.

"We're going up to claim a section of land, Cole. Devoted exclusively to a full-fledged, fully equipped astronomical observatory. The atmospheric conditions up there are ideally suited to the continuance of my cataloging of celestial phenomena. Cap and Spunky have agreed to assist me as site managers and caretakers and to help with clearing the land and with the building project. I must hurry back east to secure funding, develop construction plans, supervise outfitting and equipping the physical plant, and of the design and building of a giant and powerful telescope, the grinding and polishing of the lenses and such. I'll need graduate students to come back with me as assistant experimenters, investigators, and amanuenses! Oh, Cole, it's an exciting and magnificent prospect! To the glory of science!" Seabring gleefully rubbed his hands.

"Amen . . . what?!" Ryerson asked.

Near Spunky, Cap Donovan ran his fingers through his thick head of seventy-four-year-old silver white hair. He seemed to have hardly heard Seabring's impassioned soliloquy. "I went gold prospecting once and broke my pick. I'm ready to try again. Up on Timberlodge. Dave Nesler proved it's there. In between helping Doc, that is. But, meantime, I got an idea, Cole. You maybe hadn't planned how to get those cavalry horses back to Major Locke at Camp Walker. We three are leaving first thing in the morning for Timberlodge—gonna stop off and see Nesler. Don't believe it'll be much out of our way to drive those army horses back where they belong. Save you the extra trip."

Dr. Seabring had remained in an astronomical, daydreaming reverie. "I plan to call it . . ." He clutched his coal lapel and threw back his head proudly. ". . . Timberlodge Observatory," he declared excitedly, his foxlike eyes agleam with a wistful, faraway look.

Ryerson shot a puzzled look at Seabring. He shook his head in bewilderment. "Some folks walk different trails," he muttered, almost to himself. He turned back to Cap. "That'd be mighty helpful, Cap. Bertha and I planned to drive them back when you fellas went home. Guess now home for you won't be that far away."

"We'll all be that close—just up on Timberlodge—if you need us again, Cole," Spunky said.

"That's sure consoling, Spunky. I hope the world only had one Bad-Face Ike. But some day I might need to mount another *posse comitatus*. For the time being I may not need any more deputies. Bertha's going to pin on Cactus Jack's old badge and be my *segundo* here in town. That may seem mighty queer to you, but it's going to work. She's easier to cope with than I used to think. Maybe I've changed. Who's to say? Maybe she has. She's still very thorough. Knows how to look after a homeplace or a camp! Oh, I ain't talking marriage, but that's an unbeatable combination. And we all saw how she can shoot!

"But there's a hell of a lot more to Bertha Maguir

238

than shootin' a rifle or fixin' fine chuck on the trail. She told me once that she was brought up to be gentle and ladylike, but not soft. And you're all living witness to how she lived up to that creed out in the badlands. As I see it, for a woman, Bertha has as stout a heart as any of you stouthearted men!"

About the Author

Everything Comes to
He Who Writes
Late Career Surge
For *Epitaph* Contributor

by Robert H. Dyer
Western History Writer and Novelist

The Tombstone Epitaph, June 1992

After struggling in the world of western fiction for many years, R. C. "Dick" House is on his way to fame with publication of his fourth western novel—and a three-book contract with Pocket Books of New York.

His first novel, *So the Loud Torrent,* is a Mountain-Man yarn published by North Star Press (St. Cloud, MN) in 1977. Then came *Vengeance Mountain,* a western adventure, published by Tower Books of New York in 1980.

His third book, *The Sudden Gun,* published by M. Evans, New York, in 1991, is a marvelous western that showcases his talent with dialogue and characterization. This book is now on library shelves across the country. His fourth book, *Drumm's War,* a western army adventure done in collaboration with the late Bill Bragg of Casper, Wyoming, is set for publication later this year.

Then his agent recently sold his manuscript of

ABOUT THE AUTHOR

Trackdown at Immigrant Lake to Pocket Books. Officials of this publishing giant were so impressed with the material that they requested two additional novels based on the *Trackdown* characters. The *Trackdown* sequels are in progress as this is being written.

Born some sixty-five years ago far from the West House would come to love and write about—in Ohio—his greatest boyhood joys were reading (emphasis on westerns and historical adventures, of course), and hiking and exploring the nearby woods and farmlands.

Muzzleloaders

When he was twelve he bought a much abused Civil War musket for $2, beginning a lifelong interest in collecting and shooting muzzleloading weapons.

After army service in World War II, he attended Bowling Green State University and Kent State University in Ohio, studying journalism and public relations. His Bachelor of Arts degree was awarded at Kent in 1951. While at Kent, he was editor of the weekly *Kent Stater* and elected to the KSU journalism honorary society.

Four years on daily newspapers as reporter, photographer and editor launched a nearly forty-year career in corporate communications; writing and editing employee newspapers and magazines for such firms as the Ford Motor Company and Occidental Life of California, and then twenty-three years as employee magazine and newspaper editor for the Jet Propulsion Laboratory in Pasadena, California, explorers of deep space, affiliated with NASA and Caltech. From this he has just retired (preferring to call it a "career change").

A newly discovered asteroid has been named for him, a coworker's recognition of his long service at JPL.

Why did western fiction and not science fiction become the subject of his freelance writing? "Interpreting science and technology for a very diverse audience was a real challenge," he remarked.

"When I found time to peck away at the typewriter at home, I wanted to lose myself in a totally different world. It was there waiting for me in the Old West. But one fed off the other; my professional writing style improved as I wrote western and muzzleloading articles and vice versa."

Western Writers Stalwart

House is a longtime member of the Western Writers of America, serving as Membership Chairman, Vice President, and then President. He served several terms on the Executive Board and was editor of the association's magazine, *The Roundup,* for three years.

House and his wife, Doris, met when both were reporters for the Conneaut, Ohio, *News Herald* in 1948. They have two children, Laura and Jonathan.

A man of many interests, House sings with "The Barbershop Four" quartet. He is a "chili head," involved with cooking in and judging chili cookoffs for years. E Clampus Vitus lists him as a member, as do The Westerners and the National Muzzle-Loading Rifle Association.

Prolific Writer

Meanwhile, House has written literally hundreds of nonfiction articles and stories under his own name— as well as his nom de plume, Beau Jacques—for such magazines as *True West, Far West, Western* magazine (in Norway), *Gun Digest, Chili* magazine, *The Buckskin Report, American Rendezvous Magazine, Blackpowder Times, Then and Now, The Trade Blanket, Rendezvous Trails, Muzzle Blasts, Muzzleloader, The Backwoodsman,* and, of course, *The Tombstone Epitaph.*

He also was commissioned to write "The Saga of the Cowboy" for the premier issue of *Disney Adventures.*

In addition to writing, he enjoys primitive desert camping, music of the swing era, and traditional and contemporary jazz.

House says he got some of his best advice from the legendary A. B. "Bud" Guthrie, Jr. *(The Big Sky* and many other books).

Over drinks and smokes at Guthrie's kitchen table in his cabin near Choteau, Montana, late one night in 1970, the famous western writer told him, "You'll never hit unless you swing" (translation: "If you're going to be a writer, write!").

Guthrie also advised: "Write a good scene and much else will be forgiven you." And "The adjective is the enemy of the noun and the adverb is the enemy of every other part of speech." (Translation: "Seek unti you find the most accurate noun and the most active verb and you'll seldom need modifiers or superlatives.")

Has he applied the Guthrie principles to his work? If you haven't read a House western novel, do so. You soon may be a fan.

No one else captures the grandeur of the West — and the special men and women who tamed it — as Zane Grey does. Every page conveys the scent of sagebrush and the feel of saddle leather. Every story reveals the true Old West: where a man's actions counted, where emotions spilled out raw and honest, where challenges meant life or death, and where freedom meant no fences for white man and red man both...

ZANE GREY

The U.P. Trail

Wildfire

The Border Legion

The Desert of Wheat

The Light of Western Stars

Desert Gold

Lone Star Ranger

Heritage of the Desert

The Rainbow Trail

Riders of the Purple Sage

Completely repackaged for 1995
Published by Pocket Books

POCKET BOOKS

Now a Major Motion Picture from TriStar
Pictures Starring **SHARON STONE**
and **GENE HACKMAN**

The

QUICK

and the

DEAD

A Novel by *JACK CURTIS*
Based on a Screenplay Written by
SIMON MOORE

Available from

POCKET
BOOKS

1068